CRAWL SPACE

a novella

Steve Toase

ISBN: 978-1-68510-174-9 (trade paper)
ISBN: 978-1-68510-175-6 (ebook)
The Library of Congress Control Number has been applied for.

First printing edition: March 6, 2026
Published by JournalStone Publishing in the United States of America.
Cover Design: Mikio Murakami
Edited by Sean Leonard
Proofreading and Cover/Interior Layout by Scarlett R. Algee

JournalStone Publishing
1400 North Wood Rd.
Murphysboro, IL 62966

JournalStone books may be ordered through booksellers or by contacting:
JournalStone | www.journalstone.com

To Annie for giving me time, space and support so I can write. To Charlie for writing alongside me, and helping me stay creative. I love you both, and am very lucky to have you in my life.

CRAWL SPACE

Chapter 1
Measure and Record

With urgent hands, Rachael tore away layers of damp-softened felt to get to the capsule. This was the third cylinder she had recovered from the vacuum pipe that ended abruptly against the living room wall. The fifth they'd found across the city. So far none contained the promised letters.

"This one a dud too?"

She ignored Ben's cynicism, and ignored him leaning over her shoulder. With both hands she rattled the object. Anything fragile would have shattered years ago.

"Something in there," she said.

"Letters don't rattle, though," Ben said, reaching across her. She held the cylinder away from him.

"Maybe a duchess hid her riches. Slid her jewellery in here away from the servants. Sent it around the Rohrpost to be recovered at a later date, and forgot."

"Maybe it holds five small planets all populated by tiny orange aliens. Just open it."

She unscrewed the top and held the open end over an old, yellowed copy of *Süddeutsche*. A shower of brick dust fell out to pool in the paper's creases. She gave the cylinder a final shake. Sixteen perfect teeth of differing sizes followed, each one rolling around until it settled into place.

"Well, I wasn't expecting that," Ben said. Rachael lined them up until they formed an arc, as if the teeth had just chewed their way through the paper.

"They form an upper jaw. Not from the same person."

"You sure?"

She picked up two teeth and held them in the palm of her hand.

"This one is from a child, a milk tooth, and this one is a wisdom tooth from a fully grown adult. Different wear patterns too," she said, putting them back in order. "This one came from a heavy smoker, while this incisor has some kind of mineral accretion."

Ben pushed them out of the curve, lining them up so they touched.

"The tooth fairy's secret stash."

"A dentist's reference collection is more likely," Rachael said. She shook the tube once more. Brick dust and wet plaster cascaded onto the old newspaper.

"Maybe he was sending them to a colleague when they got diverted and caught up in the system."

"Have you measured the pipe?" she said, nodding toward the corner. The stub of pneumatic infrastructure curved up out of rotten floorboards, the walking stick-shaped terminal designed, at one time, to spit capsules onto the desk of a waiting clerk whose job it was to sort the letters. The desk was long gone, and now the rusted terminal ended in mid-air.

Ben picked up the tape measure, camera, and clipboard with an empty pro-forma sheet in place, and began the steady process of noting down the material, shape and size of the pneumatic pipe. Somewhere above them, rain found a way through the half-stripped roof, dripping down the mould-rotten wallpaper to splash on the floor.

"Why pack them with rubble?" Ben said, pausing with the hand tape bridging the entrance to the pipe.

"Probably leached in around the seal."

"Shit seal."

Rachael shrugged. The stench of damp intensified in the room.

"It's been in the ground for sixty years at least."

"Still impressive for chunks of mortar to get in, when it's been in the pipe."

"Still not letters, though."

Ben nodded.

"Still not letters."

Chapter 2
Measure Twice Cut Once

Back at the accommodation, Rachael moved the decorative miner's lamp and wooden platter from the small hotel table and laid out the day's finds. She started to make notes. Two empty capsules and the one containing teeth and rubble. Her body switched into muscle memory.

She looked in her bag for the artefact record sheets and clipped them over the top of the ones Ben had already filled in.

She took out her camera and scales and photographed the finds. First the teeth as a group, then individually, turning each one to capture accretions and damage. She checked them over for signs of drilling or scrimshaw, but found none. They were just teeth, perfect or not, as if they had fallen from jawbones that no longer wanted the extra weight. She made a rough guess as to the age of the individual (child, teen, or adult), then dropped them into a small plastic finds bag.

For a moment, it almost felt like proper archaeology. Like those evenings in the accomo processing the day's finds before the office sent someone out with shiny rigger boots and a brand-new hard hat to collect them. Checking context sheets and filling in the site diary. But it wasn't proper archaeology, and there was a huge gulf between working on Iron Age burial sites and pulling early 20th century teeth out of pipes in the ground.

She finished the paperwork and turned her attention to the capsules, lining them up and laying out the felt pads pulled away to allow access to the contents. Even without further analysis, the difference was obvious. Two were the same size, the third too large. Several centimetres bigger than the others they'd pulled from the pneumatic tube. She checked again. It was the one containing the teeth. She was not surprised by that. Atypical finds were often with other atypical finds. Flicking back through the paperwork to Ben's record sheet for the pneumatic pipe, she read the measurements. The pipe was 150mm wide, the capsule 220mm wide.

There was no way it would work within the delivery system. No way it should have ever entered, never mind come out. Definitely not part of the system. The felt was different from the other two capsules. Compact. More fur-like than felt. Smelled of wet dog. The only way it ended up in the tube was if someone dropped it down there, and even then, how did it fit? She photographed the cylinders once more and measured the dimensions to make sure she wasn't imagining the difference. There was a clear 5cm discrepancy.

Ben answered after three failed attempts to make the call.

"Are we on overtime on this job?" he said. She listened to him gulp down some kind of liquid. Checked her watch. 9pm. Probably halfway through a bottle of vodka.

"We work the job, not the hours," she said, and listened to him sigh.

"No, I'm pretty sure I work the hours. What do you want? You're cutting into my doing fuck all time."

"Are you sure you measured the pipe correctly?"

"Of course I'm sure I measured the pipe correctly. It's hardly a complicated job. Why, what's up?"

Rachael picked up the capsule, flinching at the felt's texture against her skin. She turned it over and looked inside.

"We're going to have to go back and check the measurements again tomorrow."

"We only had permission to go into the site today, and we're supposed to be visiting the next location tomorrow."

"BerringStrasse?"

"That's the one."

"They're not far apart. We'll go back. Do a couple of quick measurements."

"If we don't get caught. And we're meeting Herr Bettelmein in the morning."

"Oh fuck. And he'll want a progress report. I don't want to say anything until we're sure of what we've found, and even then we haven't found what they've employed us to look for."

"So keep our mouths shut."

"It's often for the best."

"So you say. I'll meet you at the offices in the morning. I don't need a wake-up call, before you ask."

Rachael tossed the phone onto her bed and picked up the capsule once more, turning it this way and that. No way the container should have fit into the system. She looked once more at the teeth and shuddered.

Chapter 3
Top Floor

The office was on the top floor of the building looking down on the tramlines that crisscrossed the street like fishing nets. Ben stayed by the window, staring at the echoes of traffic in the street. The comings and goings of the buses that disgorged people onto the already crowded pavements. He shifted the equipment bag on his shoulder and leaned against the glass as if his eyesight was failing him in the early morning light. Rachael sat in the chair in front of the desk, bag by her foot and a cup of cooling coffee balanced on her lap. The door opened and Rachael stood out of habit, balancing the cup and saucer on the edge of the desk.

Herr Bettelmein was an imposing man. Six foot three with a shock of red hair that curled over his collar, obscuring several scars she did not know him well enough to ask about.

"Frau Jenson. Good to see you," he said, reaching out and enveloping her hand like some kind of sea creature devouring its prey. "I trust you are keeping well, and the accommodation is good?"

Rachael nodded.

"Your organisation is looking after us very well. They don't seem to mind us littering their rooms with our equipment," she said, sitting once more.

"And you, Herr Caston. You, too, are happy with the accommodation? With the way you are being treated by my colleagues?"

"No complaints so far," Ben said.

Herr Bettelmein narrowed his eyes, as if considering what he would do if there were any complaints, then smiled. "I am sorry that we could not place you in the same pension, but as I'm sure you understand, at this time of year accommodation is scarce." He waited until they both nodded, then continued. "If I'm truthful, and I do like to speak the truth, there is never a time when accommodation is easy to come by. Oktoberfest, Christmas Markets, summer holidays. The city is always full."

He sat down in the chair, an act that seemed to Rachael certain to end with the furniture crushed to powder.

"It's perfectly fine," Ben said. "After a day working together, a break from each other for the evening is refreshing."

"I'm glad to hear it. I invited you here because, frankly, I expected more progress," he said, leaning forward on the desk. "I understood that you had undertaken this type of work in both London and Paris with very successful results."

"Our track record is impeccable, and yes, we are making progress, but it is slight."

"And would there be any reason for that beyond simple incompetence?"

Ben went to speak and Rachael held up her hand to stop him. She did not miss the smile that crossed Herr Bettelmein's face.

"Part of the issue, Herr Bettelmein, is the strength of the German privacy laws that make it very difficult to access the tube terminals located on private property. This means that the number of sites we can visit is very limited. Also, these are historical features. Survivors of the many vagaries of progress. This means that methods of recovering contents from the tubes are limited. There are techniques, but they can be fairly destructive to the historical record, so I want to keep those in reserve."

"You are correct that us Germans do value our privacy, but I think the lack of the results over the last two weeks mean that we—or you, more precisely—might need to rethink approaches. We can certainly arrange to ease access to private property. Our organisation can be fairly persuasive if need be."

Rachael shook her head.

"We still have three properties to investigate that fall into the derelict category. If those prove fruitless, then we will consider other options." She had no doubt that Herr Bettelmein's methods would not be pleasant for the homeowners, and they would be unwelcome guests anywhere Herr Bettelmein's organisation helped them enter.

"Then maybe you need to consider your methodology, Frau Jenson. You realise that this is a time-limited issue? Yesterday you were at," he paused to look at a sheet of paper on his desk, "Schneebahn Straße." Neither she nor Ben had told Herr Bettelmein's colleagues where they were working.

"That's correct."

"And did that prove fruitful at all?"

"We found two cylinders. Both empty."

"That is a shame. I hope we can continue to work with you. Your previous projects appear to be of the highest quality. You trained as an archaeologist, yes?"

"And worked as one for a decade before a sideways move into this more specialised field."

He pulled a file toward him across the desk and opened the cover, flicking through the sheets of paper. Rachael saw the crest of her old university and a photocopy of her passport before their employer closed the cardboard over, placing both hands on top.

"Was there any particular reason you moved from the more mainstream profession into something so..." He paused. "Precise?"

"Those three old things," Ben said. "Money, job security, and a need to eat regularly."

Herr Bettelmein stared at Rachael.

"Your colleague has a sense of humour. I do like jokes. In their place."

"He does have a sense of humour," Rachael said, breaking the man's gaze to scowl at Ben. "But on this occasion, he is telling the truth. We moved into setting up our partnership due to the lack of work during the downturn. Once we made our name, it turned out there was no one else involved in the type of investigations we were pursuing. Mr Bettelmein, can I be candid?"

"Please do. I respect candour. And honesty."

"I really wish you'd called us in earlier. I'm reluctant to use methods that are destructive to the historical remains. It goes against several principles of our business."

"We only found out two months ago that these legal letters had entered the Rohrpost system, and that there was a strong likelihood that they were lost within the network of pipes. And when it comes to principles, in the market I always find it's good to have principles that are flexible."

"We will do our best to work for a positive outcome, Herr Bettelmein."

"That would be in all our interests," he said, standing up. "Frau Jenson. Herr Caston. Please excuse me as I have other business to attend to. Finish your coffee. Don't rush on my account."

Chapter 4
Doesn't Add Up

The site was the same as when they left the previous day, even down to their footprints in the dust on the floor, the powder turned to sludge by the incessant rain. In one corner, a fatty substance weighed down some old fabric. Opposite, the pipe rose out of the floor, unchanged and static. Rachael pictured it as the maw of a many-headed insect stretching itself out under the city, growing and forcing necks through the floors of unsuspecting houses. Painted carapace instead of flaking metal.

"So we're back here because you think I made a mistake?"

"Something isn't right. It doesn't work."

"I measured it correctly."

"I have no doubt," Rachael said. She opened her bag and pulled out a paper-wrapped parcel. Removing the elastic bands, she passed him the capsule. "Measure that."

He shrugged and opened his own bag, took out a fluorescent hand tape, and measured the width and length of the object.

"440mm long and 220mm wide."

"Give me the tape."

She leaned over the pipe and measured the opening.

"170mm."

"What?"

Ben took the tape from her and measured the capsule once more, then the pipe. The measurements were correct.

"Now put the capsule into the tube," she said.

Ben looked from the capsule to the corner of the room, then to her.

"Not the whole way, obviously. Just slide in the first third."

Ben gripped the capsule as if expecting resistance, then watched the object slide inside the pipe.

"That's not possible."

"And yet we've both stood here and watched it happen. Take a photo of the capsule part way in, then we best leave before someone complains."

Ben went back into the bag and brought out the site camera. She watched him try and hold the capsule in place and take the photo with his free hand.

"Let me," she said, taking the camera off him. "Hold the tape in place."

The numbered yellow tongue flicked out over the unfelted end and the metal L hooked over the edge. Making its own decisions, the camera flicked out its flash and she waited while the lens focussed itself, taking several shots, while she luxuriated in the indulgence of endless storage memory.

She brought up the images to check the numbers were in focus and zoomed in on the intersection between pipe and container.

"Can I move yet, or do you want me to stay here for a bit longer?"

"Of course you can move. Why wouldn't you be able to?"

"You might have wanted to take another photo."

She stared at the corner for a moment, at the pipe where Ben's hands balanced tape and capsule.

"We'll take one of the tape across the opening, then we'll be done."

"I took one yesterday."

"I want them in sequence. Belt and braces."

Sighing, he placed the tape across and waited while she took another handful of shots, the camera responding to the gloom in the house.

"Done now."

Ben stood up and packed away the kit.

"Not before time. I don't know how often they check this place. I'm not sure I can trust Bettelmein to get us out of custody."

"He's not that bad. Just a bit certain about what he wants."

"And we're not going to present that to him if we get distracted by odd stuff like this. It's not their lost letters, is it?"

"They might be funding the investigation, but I'm going to record what we encounter."

"Just in case the Institute of Field Pneumatic Post Investigators throws you out for bringing the profession into disrepute?"

"Pack your stuff. We need to get out of here." The mould-heavy air wrapped around her tongue and she couldn't stay in the room any longer. Shouldering her bag, she opened the broken front door, walked into the yard, and lit a fresh cigarette.

The man stood on the corner of the street, his hands both pushed inside the folds of his coat. His clothing looked out of place, even on such a damp day, the heavy woollen cap and great coat. Scars ran from corners of his mouth to the corners of his eyes like some kind of ventriloquist doll. She tapped ash into the puddles around her feet and tried to look away, but knew he was still watching. She finished smoking and let the filter fall to come apart. Across the road, the man opened his mouth and smiled, livid red gums empty of teeth like raw, unscabbed wounds.

"This is where we're going next," Ben said, shoving the phone under her face, the red point blipping on the map. Rachael looked up and the man on the corner was gone.

"Eisenbahn?" she said, opening the gate and looking up and down the street.

"Always," Ben said.

The tram was crowded and hot and there was nowhere to sit down. They shuddered across the city, watching families struggle on and off with pushchairs, drunks trying to get the attention of anyone whether they cared or not. Above their heads, the electronic screen shifted to show their destination. They forced their way through the crowds to get closer to the door, and erupted onto the pavement.

"Five minutes' walk," said Ben, looking at his phone.

"Just nice to be out of the crush."

"I felt like a letter from 1922."

"Damp and curled around the edges?"

"That's pretty much it."

Chapter 5
Rats

They walked in silence, searching the street numbers for the right building.

"BerringStr. 42. There it is."

The building was down an alley in a small square, the centre dominated by a metal sculpture of three bears fighting. Rachael walked up the steps and rang the first bell.

"Hallo?"

In halting German, she explained who they were and held the letter up to the small, discreet camera.

"Kommt," the speaker said, and somewhere down the side of the door an electronic switch operated, letting her press it forward.

The Hausmeister stood just inside the door. He was in his fifties and worn, lank grey hair obscuring his face.

"We're here to look at the remains of the Rohrpost system," Ben said, holding out his hand. The man ignored it and continued staring at Rachael.

"Permission letter, please," he said.

She took the piece of paper out of her pocket and gave it to him, watching him unfold it slowly and scan each word from the address to the signature.

"You're working for the Durchsickern Institute?"

"They are a major funder of this particular research project, but we are an independent company."

"I remember the Durchsickern Institute from when I worked on the railways. They funded research then too." He folded the letter up and held it out for Rachael. "This way, please."

Pausing while he activated the lights, they followed him down a short staircase to a landing, and waited once more while he searched for the switch just inside the cellar.

The vast space was dominated by wood and wire cages, containing forgotten possessions of the residents in the building above. Bikes with half-inflated tyres pushed up against empty Lego boxes hoarded with some vague hope of repackaging the sets once children had grown. Clothes scented with damp covered unused barbeques and piles of baby toys no one had played with in that decade.

Walking slowly, the Hausmeister led them to a far corner and waved his hand to get them to move back as he unlocked the padlock.

"Is this your storage space?" Ben said. Rachael always forgot how allergic he was to silence.

"This one belongs to no one. It contains these stumps and none of the residents wanted to use it in case rats crawled up to feast on their precious stuff."

Rachael shook her head.

"Rats don't use the pneumatic tubes. They're steel and most are blocked by forgotten capsules."

The Hausmeister wiped his face. Reaching into his pocket, he took out a half-smoked cigarette and slid it into the gap where an incisor should be.

"You don't know rats, Frau?"

"Jenson," she said.

"If you need anything, just ring the bell for Apartment Four. I am going to eat now."

Rachael nodded and waited until he left before taking off her rucksack.

"Is that true? Rats don't use the pipes?" Ben said when the Hausmeister was out of earshot.

"I've never found any evidence of them, and I've peered down a few more of these things than that creepy fuck. Can you get the endoscope ready?"

Ben dropped his bag and took out the camera, unfurling the segmented cable. They had worked together in three countries now and she was alert, watching for the shifting point. The moment in the project when the stress of not being home got too much and the evening beers got too plentiful. His hands were steady as he went through the checking procedure. She took out her camera and photographed the terminals before they got started.

The pipes would have originally extended right across the room, or maybe up through the ceiling of the cellar. Pushing out capsule after capsule. Eggs of words and ink. In the past, someone had cut off the rest of the metalwork and capped it with discs of steel and bolts. She ran a hand across the plaster above her head, but there were no traces of where it might have pierced the architecture of the building.

From a compartment she pulled out two adjustable spanners, giving one to Ben, a small can of WD-40, and a hammer.

"You take the right and I'll take the left. Try not to shear it."

"Once. It happened once. I've not done that since Prague."

"But it was a pretty spectacular one when you did."

For the next ten minutes they worked in silence, lubricating, bashing, and spannering, until finally the panel dislodged and clattered to the floor.

The endoscope revealed nothing beyond a light coating of rust and mould from where the damp air of the cellar had found its way into the system.

"Well, that's a bust," Ben said, packing away the cable.

"Nothing at all?" Rachael asked, not quite believing him first time.

He replayed the recording of the exploration.

"Nothing at all," she said. "Let's get this recorded and onto the next one. I don't trust that Hausmeister not to lock us in this cage for his rats to feast on."

Over the next twenty minutes, they filled in pro-formas and took photos of what they hadn't found, locking the compartment behind them.

The door to Apartment Four opened and the Hausmeister stood in the way.

"Yes?"

"Just to let you know we're done."

"And you found nothing?"

"The tubes themselves are always worth recording, but nothing of any more interest lodged inside."

"So nothing to stop the rats getting through, then?" He smiled, his tongue playing with the back of his teeth.

"We replaced the metal cap so you don't need to worry about rodents getting into the cellar. Anyway, if they can get through the capsules, then your chicken wire and MDF aren't going to hold them back."

He coughed a laugh, the sound liquid and debilitating.

"Depends what you coat the chicken wire and MDF with. I'd make sure you wash your hands well before lunch. One child was playing down there and didn't. Awfully sick. Awful. Not that I felt much sympathy. The cellar is no place for a child to go poking about, is it?"

"Thank you for your help, Herr?"

"Just call me Hans."

"Is that your name?" Ben said.

"No," the Hausmeister said, slamming the door in their faces.

Rachael looked at her phone, scrolling the map to the next location.

"Eichenstrasse next. Number 43."

The next location gave up nothing, though it was derelict, which meant they didn't have to deal with any reluctant owners or Hausmeisters. The third one was a false lead, and the fourth filled with concrete only recently poured. They sat outside drinking cheap coffee out of cheap cups.

"Can we fit another one in today?" Rachael said, deciding that if Ben got her another coffee without sugar she'd use it to scorch away his face and fingerprints so the authorities couldn't identify the body.

"Really? Can't we just call it quits?"

"Look at it this way. If the trend of the day continues, there will be fuck all and I can go back to my room for a bath and a book, and you can go attempt to drink your way through the city's beer supply, or whatever you do when you're alone."

He went to speak and she put a finger to her lips.

"Don't say anything. Nothing good will come of speaking at this moment."

Her phone rang against her ribs. She held it up to read the name, rolling her eyes at the name withheld.

"Can't I even enjoy a sub-par coffee in peace?" she asked no one in particular.

"Frau Jenson. You're not an easy person to speak to."

"Herr Bettelmein. How lovely to hear your voice. We've spent most of the day in cellars or rooms like concrete bunkers, so as you can probably appreciate, a phone signal has been hard to acquire."

"If you are to work for us for much longer, Frau Jenson, we may need to work out a more efficient way of you keeping us up to date on your progress."

"Hopefully that won't be necessary, and just to clarify one minor point. We do not work for you. You are funding this particular stage of our ongoing research project because some of our goals align, but we are independent and I will keep repeating this fairly major detail until it sticks."

"Mere semantics, Frau Jenson."

"Oh, Herr Bettelmein, I can assure you that it is not mere semantics." She covered the mic, passed her cup to Ben, and whispered, "Another, and don't forget the sugar again, or we'll need the endoscope to find the cup."

"What progress have you made today?"

"We have visited four sites and nothing at any of them."

"All empty?"

"Of anything to interest you. A couple of beautiful examples of surviving early twentieth century communications infrastructure, but no, no capsules."

"You wouldn't be holding out on me, would you? The conditions of funding were quite clear."

"And we're holding up our end of the bargain, but I don't remember a clause suggesting that you could ride our back while we're trying to work. As we agreed, I'll update the shared diary at the end of each day, and you can track our progress via that."

"Of course, and my apologies," he said. She could almost hear his hands widening in contrition. "I have a personal interest in the recovery of these documents. They are...family artefacts."

"And as soon as I have anything to report, you will be the first to hear. At the moment, we have nothing. Please excuse my bluntness, but we have another site to visit today and if I don't do it now the only way I will get my colleague to go there is in chains."

"Of course. Viel Glück, Frau Jenson."

She cut off the call and cradled the phone for a moment, staring at the screen.

"Here you go."

She took the cup from Ben and sipped the liquid caffeine.

"You got it right, and you have no idea how close you came to death this afternoon."

"The rat poison thing."

"The forgetting my sugar thing. Where is the next site?"

Ben opened his phone and waved it around, trying to capture the 4G from the air.

"Twenty-minute bus ride away. Then, are we done?"

"Then, for the day we are done."

Chapter 6
On the Outside Looking In

"Are you happy doing this on full show to the street?" Ben said, opening the unlocked door to the empty store.

"Do you have a set of blinds hidden in your rucksack? Four square metres of newspaper and some wallpaper paste?"

Ben stared at her and didn't speak.

"Then we're going to be doing this on full show to the street."

The room was large and concrete, all fixtures and fittings ripped out, leaving nothing but a spread of flyers and old takeaway menus across the floor. Rachael sat cross-legged against one of the walls, took out her papers, and spread them in a semi-circle around her.

"Which one is this again?" she said.

"Tanzenbaum Straße."

"I can't find any notes on it."

"There aren't any. We nearly missed this one. It wasn't on the main plan, and it was only on some obscure map from the 1920s."

"We're sure it's viable?"

Ben pointed a small torch toward the corner of the room.

"Has some pipes to look at."

Two tubes rose out of the ground, then terminated abruptly in jagged metal as if some snaggle-toothed beast had gnawed away the above-ground section of the system.

"I'll get the endoscope down. See what we're dealing with," Ben said.

"Watch yourself on those edges. Don't want you getting tetanus and dying on me."

She wrote up the start of the recording sheet while he worked, sliding the narrow cable from the endoscope into the maw of the first tube, then the second.

"Any indication which is the in and which is the out pipe?"

"The old In-Out," Ben said, leaning over the tiny screen, his face lit by the insipid glow.

"Not appropriate. Ever," Rachael said.

"Sorry. Looks like we've got something."

The endoscope had stopped against something. Just visible on the monitor was the greyscale blur of texture. Fur or felt.

"Could be a dead rat."

"You shouldn't listen to old drunk men. And it's too flat to be a dead rat. Also, the endoscope would have slid straight into its rotten flesh."

"Do I want to know?" Ben said.

"No. No, you don't. Get the extractor out."

The extractor was a collapsible and flexible metal pole with a tripod claw on the far end, operated by a thin core cable. Keeping the endoscope in place, Ben ran the extractor alongside, using the faint image to guide the claws into place and slowly pull the object toward him. The capsule toppled from the top of the pipe onto the floor.

"Careful. They're nearly 100 years old now."

"I'll see if there's anything else in there."

She watched him run the endoscope back down the pipe, waiting until the screen resolved.

"There's at least one more in there. Do you want to open the first, or drag this one out?"

"Finder's privilege. I'll get the next one."

The next two capsules had accreted together, coming out as one piece; the following three came out singularly; another at the back was jammed in the pipe.

Tightening the jaws of the extractor, Rachael wrenched the capsule toward her, putting her foot against the concrete wall to get more grip.

"Do you need a hand?" Ben said, looking up from where he was recording the dimensions of the first container.

"I'll be fine," she said, wrapping the cable around her hand and twisting the device so the capsule would spiral away from the blockage.

The cylinder erupted from the tube, sending Rachael flying onto her back, the container clattering somewhere behind her against the door. A shower of brick fragments and wet plaster followed, as if dragged on by the removal, coating her hair and rouging her face with a powder of baked clay. Dust settled on her lips, drying up all the moisture.

"You okay?" Ben pushed her bag across the room. She took out a bag of wipes, clearing her mouth and eyes before wiping down her hands.

"I've never seen one go like that before."

"Tube still pressurised?"

"Unlikely. The pumps won't be working. Long since taken out of use. Just some kind of weird vacuum caused by so many capsules plugging up the system. How many in total?"

Her mouth tasted of damp and mould, and no matter how much she spat into the dust around her feet, the flavour didn't shift.

"Seven. All felt-coated. I'm almost finished with this one and ready to open it."

Rachael nodded and stood. The rubble was still tumbling out of the tube into a pile on the floor. She watched it carry on arriving, the stack rising and rising like the sand in a timer marking the fallowing away of life.

"We've got something," Ben said.

The letter was still in its envelope, damp inside sprouting spores along the gum of the flap and stretching the ink of the address.

"Can you make out a name?"

"Too far gone, but the contents should be in better condition. Do you want me to open it?"

"Photograph, dimensions, then very, very carefully. Clear some floor so we don't contaminate it with dirt."

He nodded and she stacked the next six containers, waiting until he finished with the camera before starting the recording process for the next one.

"There might not be rats down there, but something is making the best of it. Look." He touched his boot to the pile of rubble and something flinched away from the contact. Rachael knelt down.

"They look like worms. Pass me that knife."

"You're not going to kill them, are you?"

"They're going to die anyway. They've coated themselves in plaster dust. They'll suffocate."

She took the small metal-handled craft knife from him and pressed the blade through the first twitching column. There was no blood or smear of mucus on the blade, just more plaster dust. She looked down at the now bisected worm and watched the two halves twitch away into the large pile of dirt.

"Odd. I expected a bit of gore. Never mind, plenty of time for gore later when I get back to the hotel room."

"How do you pass your evenings?"

"Mainly watching movies that would turn your stomach. You?"

"Mainly drinking copious amounts of alcohol that would turn your stomach."

"Fair. What have you got?"

The letter was two sheets long and dated to 1926. Rachael read German better than she could speak it. Though she struggled with the handwriting and the cryptography of age, after twenty minutes she had deciphered the message and written a translation onto the recording sheet.

"Anything for Herr Bettelmein?"

"Not unless he is interested in a daughter trying to convince her parents to let her come home after her teenage romance fell apart. It's sad, it's history, but I don't think it's of interest to the Durchsickern Institute."

"What do you think they want us to find?"

"My guess? Something legal. A lost will. Deeds to a property hidden in the Rohrpost system. Accounts maybe. Not a pleading letter from a 19-year-old girl who is probably long dead by now. We'll show them for completeness, but I can't see them calling us off on the strength of this."

"Are we showing them everything?"

"At the right time. Time is everything in business."

"Shouldn't it be *timing* is everything?"

"No. Not in the slightest."

The conjoined capsules contained nothing but some broken glass and the added scent of floral perfume. The next two were empty. The last three looked different, the felting more like animal hide.

"Are you busy?" Rachael said, not looking up.

"Nothing that I can't pause."

"Measure these," she said. "Then measure the tubes."

She leaned against the wall while he worked. When she first started hunting down the pneumatic tubes, she'd worked alone, but as the business grew and the amount of equipment needed grew, it made sense to take on an assistant. And, truth be told, the isolation of new hotels and new cities and new sites, all by herself, was close to driving her into working in an office just to occasionally have a conversation, and she didn't want the deaths that would result on her conscience.

"220mm wide."

"The tubes?"

"No, these three capsules."

"And the tubes?"

"Hang on," he said. She stayed silent as he walked across the room and laid the tape as best he could across the jagged, disrupted openings.

"150mm."

"You sure?"

"Do you want to check yourself?"

"No, I trust you. What figures have you been getting for the other capsules?"

"What we'd expect. 150mm including the felt."

She dragged one of the oversized capsules across and placed it next to the normal ones. Beside each other it was obvious that they were different. That one was so much larger. Even beyond the felting, they were constructed differently. The metal a different thickness, almost flexible to the touch, and white flecks like bone inclusions in the surface.

"I want these three open now to check what's going on."

"You don't want to talk about the 70mm size discrepancy?"

"I want to talk from a place of knowledge, and at the moment that is very much not somewhere I am."

They each took one, leaving the third on the floor between them. Ben opened his first, unscrewing the lid and holding the capsule vertical for a moment before tipping the contents out onto the floor. Splinters of wall slats fell into a pile and he slowly tapped them with his boot.

"Well, that's a bit of an anticlimax."

Rachael held hers, wrapping both hands around the cold metal, then unscrewed the cap and tipped whatever was inside onto the floor.

The worms were longer this time, all knotted together like the tails of a rat king. She stepped back to avoid their squirming and watched them rapidly make their way as one mass over to the pile of rubble beside the tubes. In their progress to get back undercover, they crawled over the earlier worms, and both Rachael and Ben watched with their hands over their mouths as the large mass of knotted creatures ripped them apart and smeared them against the concrete.

"Did you just see that?"

Rachael nodded her head.

"Just some weird kind of underground nematode. Found a way to live in the system and not reacting well to being dragged out into the light."

"They massacred the other worms."

"I'm not sure worms have enough life to cause, or be part of, a massacre."

"Did you used to chop the heads off your dolls as a kid? Torture small animals?"

"No, just fellow students who kept annoying me. Open the third one. We need to check it. We might as well get it over and done with, then we can get out of here and eat," she said, holding her hand behind her back so Ben couldn't see her shaking.

"There's something in here," he said, holding up the capsule toward her.

"More rubble, or weird underground fauna?"

"It looks like some kind of legal document, but it's so covered in dust I can't make out the details."

Rachael brushed away the dirt and took a couple of record shots, flicking through the photos to check the detail she could not see in the brief camera flash.

"Look." The words were faded and smeared with white cement, but legible.

"Durchsickern Institut."

The movement outside the window made her look up. She had forgotten they were on full display, so caught up in getting the job done and getting out of the shop that she hadn't cared about anyone staring in while they worked. The woman was younger than Rachael, neat corporate hair tied back and kept dry under a woollen hat. Her suit cuffs were soaked by the unending rain where she held her hand up to peer through the window, her breath misting the glass. Noticing Rachael looking, she stepped back and smiled, and Rachael saw the small gap where one of her front teeth was missing.

#

"Do you work for Bettelmein?" Rachael said, standing in front of the woman.

The woman pressed her hands into her pockets and continued smiling, her mouth evolving to a tight closed-mouthed smile.

"Because you can tell him I don't appreciate being spied upon, especially as your organisation does it so fucking incompetently."

The woman's smile widened again, showing her incisors. With thin, arthritis-spun fingers, she reached between her jaws and pulled her teeth out one by one, bloody roots staining her velvet gloves. Still she said nothing to Rachael.

"Just tell him to leave us to do our job."

Inside the shop, Ben sat staring at the book. She sat down beside him. The spasms at the sight of the flesh-encrusted enamel shuddered up her gullet and came out as a retching she couldn't mask.

"You okay?"

She shook her head.

"One of the reasons I started working by myself." Ben looked up at her with a hurt look on his face. "For myself," she corrected, "was so I wasn't under surveillance of some boss. Fucking helicopter management."

"We all have to answer to someone."

"If I do a good job, they pay me. If I don't, they don't. There is no need for them to send out their employees to watch what we're doing."

Her phone started to vibrate in her pocket.

"And as if on cue."

She sat down in the corner and pressed the green handset button.

"I'm not impressed, Herr Bettelmein."

"Your British manners seem somewhat lacking."

"Your hospitality also. Please don't send your employees to spy on my work, and if you really can't help yourself, at least send one who can manage to be discreet."

"I apologise that my associates have interrupted your progress. Herr Stein is normally very talented at not getting seen."

"What do you want, Herr Bettelmein?"

"I believe that you've found some evidence pertinent to our contract."

She stared at the floor in front of Ben. The booklet lay on the floor, protected from further dirt by a sheet of A4 paper, a small photo scale along the top edge.

"We have one find that may be of interest. Once we have recorded it fully and assessed it for any conservation risks, I'll be more than glad to show you."

"My associate Herr Stein will bring you into my office in one hour. Please make sure you have finished your work for the day by the time he finishes his coffee and walks across to meet you."

"And how will I know the mysterious Herr Stein?"

"You'll know him."

Ben looked up with the camera loose in one hand.

"Trouble at the mill?"

"There might not be a mill left standing to have trouble at if this approach continues."

Chapter 7
This Way, Please

Herr Stein was not a woman with all her teeth pulled out at the root.

"The car is just down here," he said in perfect English. "You will have to excuse me for not introducing myself earlier, but it is often necessary that I keep a distance from Herr Bettelmein's contractors."

Ben looked the man up and down.

"It might be worth keeping that distance for the foreseeable future. My boss is not happy with your boss's tactics."

Rachael climbed into the back beside Ben and stared straight ahead. He tapped her on the arm and turned his phone to her.

You OK? it said, the text blinking out. She shrugged and stared out of the window while they waited for the traffic to clear and give them space to pull into the road. On the pavement she thought she saw a flash of blood before the car turned past a tram and into the lane.

"I understand you've been here before and know your way up to the office."

Rachael walked inside.

"Are you not joining us to make a report to your boss?"

"I've already reported what I need to do. He likes to be kept up to date much more regularly than a single summary."

"And the woman? Does she report to you or directly to Bettelmein?"

Herr Stein looked confused for a moment.

"Of course, it's not impossible he sent two teams, but for a surveillance job like this, one person is normally sufficient."

"And you've been following us all the time, or do you work in shifts? Have you been in our rooms? Bugged our phones?"

"Look, if the job requires that close scrutiny, then that is the type of work my branch of the Institute will undertake. For someone like yourself scratching around in the dirt, think of me as a daily diary. A progress report so that you have less paperwork to deal with."

She leaned in close to his face, not really caring about his personal space or the PTSD she was sure he carried as an extra qualification.

"Unless you're going to turn up and actually fill out my paperwork, I'm still spending my evenings sat on my bed, drinking coffee and writing up fucking notes. On top of that, I seem to get summoned here far more often than I think I would if you weren't puppy-dogging us around during our work days."

He smiled, his breath strong with some kind of herbal tea.

"On that you're mistaken. If I wasn't following you around, you would be ringing in approximately every two hours, sending photos every three, and possibly worrying about a dear relative getting fed by the polite but firm gentlemen who had moved into their spare room. After you, Frau Jenson."

Herr Bettelmein sat behind his desk, a spread of papers across the leather top, under his elbows and wide-spread hands. Something unsettled her about the way his workspace was set up. It had last time. She realised it was the lack of a screen. His desk was completely clear of monitors, laptops, tablets, or mobiles. There was nothing there apart from sheets of paper and a single uncapped pen that was worth far more than any of the specialist equipment she had taken out several bank loans to purchase.

He looked up. Sweat hung on his brow, and his palms left imprints on the leather-topped table as he shifted paper around in some kind of administrative puzzle she could not understand.

"I believe today was more successful," he said after a pause.

"Four sites, three failures, but the last one was profitable."

He held out his hand, still only reaching halfway across his vast desk.

"The book, please," he said. It was not a request. There was no chance or opportunity for her to disagree or refuse. She reached into the bag and handed over the book.

He placed it on the papers in front of him. For such a neat, refined man, she was surprised he was not distressed at the brick dust grinding into his documents.

"And who discovered this?"

"I pulled the capsule from the pipe. Ben opened it and identified the name on the front."

She turned around. Ben squatted in the far corner, his work bag in front of him, staring up at her.

"There will be a bonus for this. You can split it between you."

"Is this the conclusion of your interest in our work?"

The laugh threw Herr Bettelmein's head back in a neck-cracking arc.

"After the money we invested? Not at all. This is significant, but not the focus of my interests. This is merely a crumb when what we are searching for, what you are searching for, is the bread store. The bakery, even."

He pushed himself upward out of the chair and walked around the desk, leaning on its gold inlaid edge. She watched the wood flex with his additional weight.

"Do you know how to find the main depot? The crossing point?"

"Of course. I've done it in three cities. I can point to it on a map for you, but it was destroyed, either by war or the development that followed."

Herr Bettelmein shook his head.

"While you've been scrabbling around underground, I've been doing research of my own. We believe that it is still…" he paused, searching for the word, "extant."

Rachael dragged her bag across the room and opened the flap, pulling out the printout of the old map.

"It's not precise enough. I can tell you it's somewhere on that block, if it survived, but there's no way we can negotiate permission to access all those buildings in time to complete the work."

Reaching behind him, Herr Bettelmein handed her the papers that covered his desks. Even with her limited German, she could see what they were.

"You bought all the buildings?"

"Through different sub-companies and individuals who help us with these particular matters, but yes, you now have access to all the buildings and can now concentrate your search there. I'm sure you can complete the next stage of your investigation in a reasonable timeframe."

She nodded.

"With access in place, then, of course. The search is much simpler. Was this always your plan?"

He took back the deeds and notary documents, chucking them behind him as if they were little more than a free newspaper pulled sodden from a letterbox.

"Once we knew you had found the booklet, it became a good business decision to ease your work."

In her head, Rachael calculated the time passed since they found the capsule until the point they were stood in the office. Her head hurt.

"Why don't you use your own people for this? You're obviously not short of resources."

"You would talk yourself out of work, Frau Jenson?"

"Not at all, but I'm a little unclear. You can buy up five buildings in less than two hours, but you want to use a small-scale contractor to carry out your research?"

"Peter, do you still have a copy of Frau Jenson's file on you?"

"The one you gave me to familiarise myself with her work patterns? Of course."

Herr Stein peeled himself away from the wall and reached inside his coat. Rachael noticed something dried at the corner of his mouth, brown and scabbed like blood. Seeing her stare, he took a handkerchief from his pocket and scrubbed his lips until the matter stained the cotton instead. From an inside pocket, Herr Bettelmein took out a pair of reading glasses.

"Graduated Bournemouth University HND in Practical Archaeology with distinction 1998, University of Bradford BSc in Archaeological Sciences 2.1 2001. Joined the Institute for Archaeologists, rising to MIFA. Four years working short-term contracts for various archaeological contractors around the United Kingdom, rising to the level of supervisor, before returning to University of York to gain your MA, which you did, again with distinction."

"I'm familiar with my own CV, Herr Bettelmein."

He held up a hand to silence her.

"Please, don't interrupt. It's very bad manners, and I expect better from the English, who are so respected for their manners. After your MA, you went back into contract archaeology. You then worked on a site called Bastion Heath, where the project manager was found to be taking bribes from the developer in exchange for scraping the site. He, of course, managed to transfer the blame to a lesser member of staff, which was you. You were stripped of your MIFA status, and while you were able to keep your qualifications, you were unable to work in British field archaeology, so you moved into the related discipline of investigating and recording vacuum postal systems."

"Is this moving towards some kind of conclusion?"

"Frau Jenson, let me be clear. A lot of people work for me, and many of them probably have a skill set that would allow them to carry out the work I'm employing you and your beer-loving colleague for. What none of them have is that skill set *and* the miasma of scandal hanging around them, which would make them far more likely to know exactly what to do, and unlikely to want to draw too much attention to themselves. I don't like attention. Not the kind this type of operation would bring. So for that reason, I would rather employ a tainted external contractor like yourself than some minion."

Rachael thought about that word. *Tainted.* It stuck in her head like a barb. The taint of scandal, of professional misconduct. The taint of mould and damp underground. The taint of rubble and destruction. The taint of public embarrassment. She looked down at her hands as if for a spot to wash away.

"When do you want us to start?"

"You will start tonight. Peter will provide you with keys to access all the buildings, and credentials if any of the residents question your presence. Of course, you will not mention the Durchsickern Institute during any further investigations."

"I had plans tonight," Ben said, shouldering his bag. "Rachael, you never mentioned overtime."

"And yet you still do it by coming here," Herr Bettelmein said. "The beer will still be there in the morning. The whiskey will be bottled, and the wine will be in the cellar. Your alcohol habit only has to wait a few hours until it can be satisfied."

"Rachael, are you really happy for him to order us about like we're employees?"

She had never shown Ben the accounts. They had worked together a lot over the years. Known each other in the late nineties when they were both students. But this was her business, and he would want to make decisions or offer advice. She wanted neither. He did not know how much of her income for the year was tied up in the bank transfers from the Durchsickern Institute. Now was still not the right time to tell him.

"Go back to your hotel room," she said. "Freshen up. Have some dinner. Finish off your paperwork, and meet me at the first building in three hours. Bring me some food. I'll pay you for that time and the rest of the evening."

Ben did not look convinced, and for a moment she thought he was going to press the point, but he slumped, and what little fight he had went out of him.

Chapter 8
The Centre Cannot Hold

The square smelled of rotten fruit in the bio rubbish bin, drifting across the small patch of cobbles and grass at the centre of the building. She looked up at the stack of flats and wondered if any of the residents knew they had a new landlord who had no interest in what was going on in their lives, in their comfort, or even in their rent, but in owning the places they called home just to ease access to what lay beneath them. She watched lights flick on, people walk past opened curtains, and others sit down to eat, all as oblivious to the world outside as the world outside was to them.

Maybe, if things had been different, she'd have been sat down in a place like this with a family. A kid getting ready for bed or a husband working late. She stared at her feet, the toecaps of her boots still stained with the rouge of broken bricks. Fuck it. No point in waiting for Ben. She might as well get started.

The key opened the door first time, and crossing the entrance hall she let herself down into the cellar. Silvered pipes of the central heating system lined the wall like some kind of cheap effect in a sci-fi movie. She reached up to run her hand along them and feel the heat, but they were too well insulated. A closed system that kept everything in. When she first talked about setting up on her own, a friend asked if she was going to just focus on the vacuum systems, or if she would expand into drains and guttering. Maybe central heating or plumbing. Now, standing in a block of flats in Southern Germany, working for a customer who had too much money and limitless influence, yet still wanted her to do the work? Something more mundane didn't sound like a bad idea.

The stairs twisted to the right and she turned on the light. The cellar was empty. None of the storage seen elsewhere. Just vast concrete walls lined with pipes and cables, occasionally broken up by functional-looking service doors. She looked back up the stairs in case Ben was standing at the top, and opened the first one.

The door was unlocked, the edges taped in yellow and black. She moved out of the way as it swung toward her and reached inside, feeling around for a lightswitch. Finding none, she turned on a torch and stepped inside.

The corridor was barely high enough for her to stand up in. If she'd worn a hard hat as she was supposed to, there was no way she could have comfortably walked inside. The walls were close enough that she placed a hand on each, both warm to the touch. There was no graffiti or service marks, no buckets stacked up in the corner and forgotten about. Just plain concrete walls and a plain concrete floor that sloped down into the darkness.

She let momentum carry her down, each step leading to the next, until she reached the end. The door was different here. Older. Made of wood and rotten, damp laminating as if the tree that gifted the timber could not escape its forest floor fate.

She pushed it away from her, then pulled it toward her. There was little give either way, the damp, swollen fittings stopping her moving into the next part of the building. Taking a step back, she kicked it away from her, not really caring about the splinters that fell off to smear across the floor. If Herr Bettelmein now owned the flats, he could stretch his budget to replace a door. She kicked again, the bottom planks falling away from the metal fittings. Reaching out, she pulled it toward her once more and stepped inside.

#

She didn't recognise any of the cigarette brands the shop on the corner sold, but she didn't care. It had been ten years since she last smoked. The flavour tasted wrong, but the nicotine did its job.

Chapter 9
Too Much

"Bad habit, that. You'll get cancer."

Rachael looked up and stubbed the cigarette out on the wet soil of the flowerbed.

"Not from one I won't," she said, not mentioning the other three she'd smoked in quick succession. Ben shivered and sat down beside her, turning his phone on.

"*Come quick*," he read. "*We've got a job ahead of us.*"

Rachael nodded.

"Bit cryptic," he continued.

"Come with me."

Her glasses steamed with the walk from cold to hot, and she paused in the corridor, wiping the moisture from the lenses. Ben was dragging his heels and his breath stank of beer, but she had no choice other than to show him now.

"Down here," she said, opening the door in the cellar and turning on the light.

"Fuck," Ben said, and went silent.

The room was vast, nearly as big as the main cellar under the tower block. The walls were pierced by pipes crossing and curving. Underneath, sleeping buffalo of generators curved in on themselves, each one connected to a different pipe system. A respirator providing oxygen to a living system. She stood and stared, giving Ben time to try and grasp the scale of the place. It was a cathedral with the organ gutted and stretched around the walls. Light glinted off the metalwork, some shimmering dull silver, others glistening with the rich polish of brass. Not everything was perfect. Patches where moisture had found its way in transformed bare surfaces to the mutations of verdigris and rust. She let Ben's reaction feed her enthusiasm. Raise her up in this thing that should not still exist. So much of archaeology was about finding the things that should not exist, the impossible beneath her feet. But this? This was different. Those things beneath her feet were broken and discarded, warped and twisted by the passage of time. This still glistened as if the age of death had passed it over. The fire and the destruction and the rending of its metal had gone elsewhere. It was as if abandoned, ready to live again, and in this temple to these things that should not be, she was the worshipper. She was the supplicant. She would kneel and worship the survivors. The ones ignored by time, swept and hidden by the building that came once the rubble was trucked away to make new hills. She gasped again despite herself and stared around the cavern of communication. The hub, the point where all words passed through. She tasted those messages in the air, and for the first time in a long time, for the first time since she left archaeology, she felt what she was doing was worthwhile.

"I thought you said it was destroyed?" Ben said, running his hand over the brass name panel of one of the generator manufacturers.

"I thought it was. They normally get targeted." She moved a service panel and peered down one of the pneumatic tubes. The air inside smelt of sewers and damp.

"Could it be later? Built again afterwards?"

Rachael shook her head.

"They look like early AEG ones. Original technology. And over there..."

She led him around the corner. The capsules were stacked like the munitions she was sure would have destroyed this room, each one with the lid flipped open, ready to take the letters once carried in the large wooden hopper beside. It was as if the workers had stepped outside for a cigarette break, ready to return and sort the letters with nicotined fingers.

"All of them?" Ben said, picking one up and turning it over. Nothing fell out from the unclasped terminal end.

"All of them," Rachael said.

"This will take a while."

"Not so long with two of us." She tried to sound upbeat, but the enormity of the task was rising like a wave to crash over her. "Start with general photographs. Measure a sample of capsules and pipes, then we'll start checking for more letters."

"Do you think these still work?"

Rachael reached under the dusty cowling and felt around for a switch, turning the Bakelite to the left. The generator creaked and flexed against the ground bolts until somewhere deep inside a flywheel rotated and air pushed through the pipes running from its core. She turned it off again.

"Now, if we can get it to suck instead of blow. Draw all the lost capsules back here. That would make life a lot easier," Ben said.

"Life is never easy. You should know that by now. Photograph everything."

They worked silently, each falling into their roles. Split the room between them, and took record shots of every piece of equipment, first with the digital cameras, then back-ups with phone cameras. Belt and braces. Every joint, every capsule, every pipe, every generator.

Ben came back with a bag full of drinks and snacks, and Rachael stood in the middle of the room, looking around at the pipes and capsules stacked against the walls. The letters, if they found any, were Herr Bettelmein's, but the information, the history, the connections and jointed links to the rest of the network, the insight? That was all hers to hold in her head, in her notebooks, in her hand. No amount of his money could possess that, prise it away from her. Let him have his mildewed artefacts. Her reward was the connective tissue that helped her draw these systems together. See the similarities. See the differences. Craft something new from those insights.

She drained the bottle and stood it against a concrete plinth holding two large compressors. Ants crawled out of the join with the floor and ringed the cap, sipping up the fruit juices that clogged up the glass. She watched the insects climb over each other, drawn by the lure of the sugar in the liquid. She waited to see where they would go, streaming back down the floor to enter once more the gap in the floor.

"Something's not adding up again."

Ben stood behind her holding two capsules in his hand.

"170mm," he said, lifting the right in the air. "While this one is 220mm, but watch."

First he put the 170mm cylinder into a pipe, watching the felt seal the gap between the two sheets of metal; then he removed it and slid in the second, larger, object. The fit was the same, engineered and precise.

"I measured across the pipe," he said.

"And?"

"Do you need me to say?"

"I need to hear."

"The pipe is 170mm. There is no question that that larger capsule should not fit into that pipe."

"And yet it does."

Rachael saw something deform her plans for pinning the knowledge down to the page. Inconsistencies. Contradictions. Yet, maybe they gave the ideas shape. Opened up new areas for her to explore.

"How long are we going to be working tonight?"

"How long can you keep going?"

"Maybe another hour," he said, yawning as if discussing the topic had reminded him how tired he was. She sat down on the floor and started to search her bag for her wide-angle lens.

"Then you do another hour and I'll see you in the morning."

Chapter 10
Alone

Having Ben there had helped her absorb the enormity of the task ahead of them, but once he left, she could start to appreciate the detail, the complexity and beauty of the engineering. The way the tubes cleared each other as they rose into the walls. She wondered how much survived beyond the concrete, and how much had been removed following the abandonment. Whether the tubes ended in stubs out of sight behind the walls, or if they snaked their way under the city, beneath houses where families slept and shops where stacked food waited unsold.

Her hand traced the cotton-wrapped power cable tailing away from one of the compressors, letting the black and white geometric wrap play between her fingers. This, too, disappeared below the ground, anchored with metal connections somewhere out of sight.

The Bakelite button turned easily and she was surprised that the motor made little more than a hum as it came to life, the pressure building behind the valve, waiting until someone turned the lock to release the air into the network of tubes.

She felt the atmosphere in the room change, as if the small amount of ozone formed around the connectors sent an electrical charge out through the concrete. There was dust on her tongue and lips. Her hand was on the second Bakelite switch. The one that would bring the whole system to life.

Deep in her pocket her phone rang, and she hesitated. The message was from Ben. Two words. *Come quick.*

Chapter 11
Come Quick

The receptionist took a moment's convincing, particularly as it was so late, or early, depending on whether your work was beginning or ending, but eventually let Rachael past the desk and up to Ben's room.

She knocked, and when there was no answer opened the door. The bed was empty, not slept in, and from somewhere farther inside she heard running water.

"Ben," she shouted in a low voice, conscious of the late hour. There was a metallic scent to the air. Not the invigorated tang of the vacuum hub, but a copper taste that made her want to spit.

He was sitting on the floor of the bathroom, holding his hands under his mouth to catch the blood clotting on his fingers. The taps were running in the sink, swirling around the porcelain and down the plughole.

"They took them all. Every single one."

His voice sounded wrong, muffled, as if cotton wool was rammed between his tongue and the roof of his mouth. She stepped over the nest of balled-up tissue paper, each sheet browned with drying blood.

"They took what? Your money?"

Slowly he opened his mouth and she saw. His voice was not muffled because of addition, but lack. Each tooth had been pulled away from his jaw carefully. No broken fragments or damaged roots remained. He spat into his cupped palms and poured the mess of blood and spit into the sink, then opened his mouth wider than any smile.

Every single one was gone. Wisdom teeth, incisors, molars. All wrenched free.

"We need to get you to the doctors."

"No, there's nothing that they can do, and they'll think I've pulled them out myself."

That thought hadn't occurred to Rachael, and she looked around the room just in case. They may have been there. Even two full jaws of teeth were easy to hide, but from his anger and self-pity, this seemed like something inflicted rather than self-inflicted.

"They obviously didn't do this in a clinic, so there's a chance of infection. You need to be seen by a doctor. At least so they can clean it up and check for damage."

She turned on the nearest tap, the cold, and waited for something to happen. For a moment nothing, then powder. Fine cement powder that tumbled into the bowl and mixed with the watered-down blood. Something skittered through the mess, leaving a dark red trail as it squirmed to the plughole, then another, until there was just the mess Ben had spat out to leave him space to talk.

"At least clean me up first."

Sleep scowled her eyes into tear-filled, unfocussed balls of dust, but she did what was needed. First she went back down to reception and got the limited first aid kit, everything out of date by at least a decade, and swilled out his mouth, stemming the bleeding with gauze, and waiting until his mouth dried before checking each fleshed curled hole in his jaw in turn. Then, searching for the nearest A&E department, she called a cab and bundled him in the back, sitting beside him while the driver took them through the late-night city in a silence she needed.

Ben did his best to keep silent, but the ache was palatable, and Rachael felt it by proxy. She held him in a way that held no affection, but hopefully calmed him in a way usually only whiskey could, and kept looking out the window until they pulled up into the entrance for the A&E.

"Leave me here. I'll be okay. I'll ring you once I've been seen."

His voice still sounded wrong, as if the words were tied back with cotton and had to fight their way through to be formed. She squeezed his arm and walked out, ignoring the taxi waiting for its next pickup, and walked back through the silent city.

Getting back to her own room, she sat by the window and watched the streets come alive. The hotel was right on the edge of the city centre and was a point from which the population spread in, filling in the blank spaces between the buildings, drawing more and more people behind them. She boiled the small plastic kettle provided by the hotel and made an herbal tea with the tag torn off that she could not identify, and when she was halfway down the cup she slept in the chair, with her legs cramped underneath her, and the rising sun in front of her, and when she dreamt it was of blood and powder and things that ached and writhed in the dirt that they were made from.

When she woke there was silence, and for a moment she thought she was still floating in a sea of slaked lime, the dust accreting to her limbs and burning. There was nothing but the faint sunlight coming through the window and the faded sound of footsteps outside.

She sat up and tried to stretch out the cramp from her legs. Ben never gave her the full story. Never told her about how he came to be attacked or lose all his teeth. Was it a random attack? Some kind of mugging gone wrong? Had they tortured him to find out something? It seemed a bit extreme to get a PIN number for the ATM. Maybe it was connected to the project. Maybe it was Herr Bettelmein trying to apply some pressure. But for what end? She searched her pockets for her phone and spotted it on the bed, a single red light embedded in the side blinking to tell her a message waited.

"They're keeping me in overnight. Can you bring my documents so that I don't have to pay?"

Chapter 12
Recovery

"The damage is very precise, but quite extensive," the nurse said, walking Rachael through the A&E to the wards behind.

"All his teeth?"

"Every single one."

"Has he said anything about what happened?"

"Nothing to any of our staff, but obviously we've been encouraging him not to talk," she said. She held the door open for Rachael. Her ID badge had her name and position, though Rachael's German was not good enough for her to translate it as they walked.

"And how long does he need to stay in?"

"He can go home now. There's nothing else we can do. It will require extensive reconstruction, as you can appreciate, but we would recommend that this is done in the United Kingdom by his own dentist."

"And you said the damage is very precise."

The nurse shook her head.

"It's the lack of damage that hints to the precision. At certain times of the year, this is a drinking town. We have a lot of injuries from fights, and as I'm sure you can appreciate, a lot of these are broken teeth, or such injuries."

"Of course."

"In those cases, the teeth tend to be broken, partially left in. There's broken enamel, often with the teeth swallowed. With your colleague, whoever did this was trained, and had experience working as a dentist. The exact removal, even the cuts to extract the wisdom teeth, is entirely typical of what we would expect to see in a patient after they leave surgery. The only stage they omitted was the aftercare."

"And the anaesthetic."

"So we're led to believe, which must have been excruciating to have all the teeth extracted in this way."

"And they were all removed."

"Every single one."

"Like a coming of age or wedding present."

"I'm sorry?" The nurse stopped, looking confused.

Rachael smiled, then stopped as if she felt she was doing it to show her own intact teeth.

"In England in the early part of the twentieth century, parents would often pay for young girls to have all their teeth removed as a gift."

"As a gift?"

"Dental care was still fairly poor, and it was felt better to have all of them extracted than deal with dental pain or decay later."

"Other countries have such strange practices."

"I'm sure your own country has its fair share."

The nurse smiled once more and opened the door to Ben's room.

"I'm sure we do. Herr Caston is in the end bed. He might not be able to talk, but he still seems able to type on his phone."

Ben was sat up in bed, his bare feet pressed against the white metal of the bed frame. The entertainment screen was swung across the bed, but he was paying it no attention, instead focussing on the smaller screen in his hand. There were two other men in the room, both sleeping. She grabbed a chair from beside the door, letting the weight swing against her wrist.

"Morning, Ben," she said. "I would have brought grapes, but I didn't think that would be appropriate, and the ice cream melted before I got here."

He typed something into the phone and turned the front toward her.

Ate it all before you got here, I bet.

"Because ice cream at ten am is entirely my style. How are you feeling?" she asked, leaning forward with her elbows on the mattress. This time he shrugged, but she watched his eyes, and looked for what he tried to hide.

"Are you still in pain?"

He opened his mouth and she saw the cotton pads in place to stem the last of the bleeding, stitches just visible underneath, she guessed by the hospital rather than the attackers.

"Where did it happen?"

Hotel, he mouthed.

"Outside?"

He nodded.

"Stupid question, but did you know them?"

He shook his head with a disbelieving expression on his face.

"I'll take that as a no, then."

The room was too warm and the fabric blinds turned the daylight into a pale honey that slicked across the room and stuck to every surface. The other two bedside tables in the room were covered in flowers and cards, making Ben's look even more stark.

"I'll contact Herr Bettelmein and arrange for you to have some time off."

Ben shook his head and winced. He reached over for his phone.

I don't need my teeth or smile to take photographs and write notes, and I do need money.

"I'm sure I can arrange some sick pay."

The only sound in the room was him typing.

I don't need sick pay. We need to keep on working.

"It's a work health and safety issue."

Herr Bettelmein has ok'd it for me to carry on working on the project.

Rachael grabbed the phone from his hand and slammed it down on the side table.

"Herr Bettelmein is not in charge of this project. I am."

She left the unanswered question unsaid. Ben grabbed the phone and carried on typing.

He already knew. I'm guessing it's down to that little spy of his.

"So why haven't I heard from him?"

In her pocket, her phone started to ring.

"As if on cue."

Chapter 13
Spying is an Inelegant Word

"Why didn't you stop it?"

She let the words hang in the air between her phone and wherever Herr Bettelmein was currently. She wanted them to puncture his eardrum and crawl down his neck to razor through him.

"I was personally not there, but of course my employees would have intervened if they had witnessed an attack in progress. They arrived just after and observed him getting up and leaving the location. As he was mobile, they decided it was better not to reveal themselves."

Rachael took a large drag on her cigarette and stubbed it out on the concrete wall until red coal burnt her fingertips.

"You let a man who had just suffered a major assault get up and walk away?"

"Once again, I was not personally there, but my employees felt that any attempt to prevent Herr Caston leaving would have only traumatised him further."

"They could have called an ambulance."

"He seems to have accessed medical assistance without any help."

"He needed my help. I helped him. I found him in his hotel room covered in blood. I took him to the hospital. God knows what would have happened if they had taken his mobile phone."

At the other end of the conversation, Herr Bettelmein sighed, covered the handset, and said something to someone she could not hear.

"My apologies. While this project is of particular personal interest, the everyday business of the Institute does not slow while I speak to you."

"What do you propose to do?"

"Propose to do? Well, the attack happened in Herr Caston's own time, and while he seems like an amiable gentleman, he also strikes me as one who values his privacy. I do not think that he would appreciate a permanent member of my staff accompanying him during his down time.

I could, of course, more visually install employees with you while you work. It would allow a more direct flow of information to my office, and allow you to focus just on the more practical side of the project."

Something whirred in the back of Rachael's mind and clicked into place.

"That's not going to be possible. As you remember, the contract we signed specified complete autonomy with regular updates."

"And I would like one of those updates today."

"I will prepare one as soon as I'm happy that Ben is okay."

There was a pause and she heard more whispered conversation.

"I will arrange to send him flowers. It feels like the least I can do."

"Don't bother. He won't appreciate them. I'd say send good whiskey, but that pleasure is out of the question for the moment."

"A report today," he said.

"Later today," Rachael said, and disconnected the call.

The street was empty, but she checked anyway. There was no way he was letting her wander the city without spying on her. If it wasn't for protection, then what was the purpose? In case she was working for a third party? She had no doubt now that her emails were being monitored. Maybe they thought she was going old school. Dead drops and in-person conversations on park benches. She looked up and down the street, then walked into the café. The air smelt of espresso and fresh bread. The phone was in the corner, archaic and forgotten. Not a modern affectation. She picked up the handset and pressed in the twenty-cent coin, waiting while it connected.

"Morning, Rachael. What's the weather like there?"

"Mainly cold. Mainly wet."

"But you don't have to be outside digging anymore, so I hope you're managing to keep warm and dry. What can I help with?"

"Do you still have access to the online journal system?"

"You haven't had it since you left the profession?"

"I haven't had it since I left university. Can you look up an organisation for me? The Durchsickern Institute."

"Can you spell that for me?"

Using the phonetic alphabet, she sounded out each letter, waiting while the man at the other end noted down the words.

"Can you give me a clue what I'm looking for? Archaeology? Research institute? Government policy? Mental health care?"

"I don't know. They seem to do a lot of things, but nothing in particular. That worries me. I need to know what their main focus is."

There was a pause at the other end.

"You're working for them and you didn't do your background checks, did you?"

She shrugged, though no one could see her.

"A job is a job."

"We could get you back in, you know."

"Back into what? The country? The Christmas card list? My old childhood bedroom?"

"Well, we'd have to move out all your mother's fabric and sewing supplies for the last one, but yes, that is a possibility. I meant into academia. You just need a good research project."

"Dad, if it was as simple as that, everyone would have a PhD."

"Not everyone deserves one. You do. How do I get hold of you?"

"I'll call you. Bye, Dad. Say hi to Mum for me."

She put the handset down and let her fingers linger on the plastic for a moment longer as if it would prolong the contact, stretch a web of skin back to a life she didn't have anymore, but there was nothing apart for the silence of the conversation and the roar of the coffee machine pushing scalding water through crushed coffee beans.

Chapter 14
A Choir of Pressure

Back in her room, she sat on the edge of the bed and stared at the recovered capsules. From a distance, they all looked the same with their felt edging and clasps. Only when she closed her eyes and ran her hands over them one after the other could she tell the difference in size. Feel the variance in dimensions. The shift in size that suggested something was wrong. Still with her eyes closed, she opened the larger cylinder and reached inside. The teeth felt smooth against her skin, their different sizes obvious to the touch. Cavities and chips searched out by fingers. She let them fall and rattle back in, listening to the sound they made as they hit the bottom of the capsule. Opening her eyes, she stared at them once more. There was still a lot of work to do at the junction room, but there was now an order in her head for how that work should unfold. She opened her hard plastic suitcase, tipped her clothes out onto the bed, and loaded in the capsules and records. Leaving the room, she slid the *Do Not Disturb* card on the door handle and went down into the lobby to call a taxi.

#

Ben was sat on the flowerbed beside the door, where the only things that seemed to grow were cigarette ends. She noticed that there was more dried blood across his lips, and his cheeks were now purple with bruising.

"You should still be resting," she said, opening the door and standing aside to let him go first.

"I'd rather be making myself useful." His voice was contorted by whispers as his breath found new ways to form words unencumbered by the press of enamel.

"I don't need you keeling over from blood loss."

In the darkness of the unlit hallway, he pirouetted and came to a stop on one foot.

"I'm fine. It doesn't hurt anymore. The painkillers the hospital gave me are working like a dream." There was a slight echo to his words, as if someone else was repeating them a moment after Ben.

"Great, so instead of worrying about you falling over through your injuries, I now need to worry about you being high as a kite."

"Just like the old days on site."

Rachael shook her head.

"I never went on site out of my head. Hungover maybe, but never wrecked."

Ben laughed. It sounded like songbirds crawling over glass.

"You were the only one who didn't then, and if you think drinking until four and starting work at six was just a hangover, then you're more delusional than I thought."

She walked on in silence, turning each light on to pin the lack of words in place, opening the door to the vacuum room and standing aside to let Ben in first. She stopped him.

"Do what I say, when I say, and if I decide that you're becoming a liability, then I'm going to send you off site."

"Always the supervisor. Always trying to prove yourself to the boss," he said. His breath smelt of copper.

"Difference this time, Ben, is that I'm the boss."

He smiled. The peaks of his gums were now the highest things in his mouth. Where they had ground against each other they were red and inflamed.

"You keep telling yourself that."

Grabbing his arm, she pulled him across the room to where the capsules were stacked like munitions.

"Label each one sequentially, photograph and measure the dimensions. If any of them are in the large category, I want them moved to one side. When you're done, let me know."

They both looked at the stacks of metal cylinders.

"And while I do that, what are you going to be doing for the next three days?"

"Recording everything else," she said.

They worked in silence. Rachael stayed at the other side of the room, but made sure that she could see him without moving at all times, glancing between the pipework to see he was still doing what she asked. There was a rhythm to his movements, and after a while she stopped observing and focussed on the tasks she'd set for herself. Although they didn't number as many as the capsules, the sheer quantity of openings to the different pipes meant that she would be measuring all day. First, she flipped open the panel, then photographed, measured, and filled in a record sheet. There was pleasure in repetition, the rhythm marking the day. Most of the tubes were clean, a smell of stale air erupting from inside when opened. Others were damp, water stains up the side of the metal showing a high-water mark of historical flooding.

"How's it going?" she said, standing behind Ben. He was sat on the floor, cross-legged, a stack of capsules in front of him.

"Slowly," he said. "It's time consuming."

"But it needs doing," she said.

"I'm sure it does." Not looking up, he paused in writing. "Are you not going for a cigarette break?"

"I'm trying to give up," she lied, her hand going to the pack in her pocket.

"Good idea. That stuff will kill you. Can cause your teeth to fall out," he said, laughing at his own joke. Rachael stayed silent.

"What have you found so far?"

"Seventy-two normal. Fifteen oversized."

"These ones?" Rachael said, nodding to a stack of capsules off to one side.

"Those are the ones."

She lifted the top one and carried it across to the nearest tube terminal. Flipping back the metal panel, she slid the end of the capsule inside, bracing herself for some resistance. There was none, and the capsule slipped away from her grasp, leaving her scrabbling to catch it by the end clasp.

From her pocket she unclipped her tape measure and checked the two measurements. 170mm tube. 220mm capsule.

It was fucking impossible. On every metric or measuring system, there was no way the capsules should fit inside the pipes, and yet they did. She laid the tape across the visible end. 220mm. Then moved it down to the entrance. 170mm. Then pulled the capsule out and measured the obscured end. 220mm. Hefting the metal cylinder in one hand, she threw it across the room, watching it crumple as it hit the concrete.

Ben was off the floor and across the room before she could say anything.

"What the fuck are you doing?" He came back with the capsule cradled in his arms.

"Expressing my frustration."

"It's an historical artefact."

"It's an early twentieth century item, and we have loads of other examples."

"You can't do that. You just can't do that. What if this one is the key to the whole puzzle? What if this one is the answer?"

She took it from him and unfastened the clasp.

"See, works perfectly."

Turning it over, she tipped it onto the floor. The single tooth hit the ground and something white and fibrous crawled away under one of the compressors.

She crouched, holding the tooth between two cold fingers, turned it around, and dropped it to rattle in the capsule.

"We need to get all the compressors turned on. Now."

"You're the boss," Ben said, his words still short and thin. She wasn't. The words came from a compulsion that was not her own intention, but driven by the press of the architecture of the system around the room. The tubes and their connections, each one leading somewhere out of sight.

They moved between the machines, silent and vast as poached elephants. She let her skin linger against the cool metal of each before turning it on, the hum and the exhale of oil-tainted air. One by one. Each in turn. A choir of pressure.

"That's the last of them," Ben said.

Rachael weighed the capsule, turning it until the tooth inside rattled like some child's first musical instrument.

"Ready?" she said, though Ben was too far away to hear.

The capsule slipped easily into the tube. She sealed the door back across and flipped the switch to release the air behind. Inside its containment, the capsule found its speed and jettisoned out of sight.

The rubble trickled out, staining the top of her boots. More followed. She heard it rattle down the tube from the direction the capsule had swooped away to. Pressing against the air generated by the compressor. The noise inside rose in volume.

"Turn them off," she shouted to Ben. "Now. Turn them off now."

Across the room, Ben dived between the compressors, flicking switches and opening valves to release the pressure. Rachael reached the closest ones. Flicking them to 0. Listening to them whirr down and reset.

The panel opened easily. Rubble and dust filling the tube to the top tipped out in a constant stream, spreading across the floor as if each particle of brick and mortar was trying to expel itself from the room. She watched it continue to pour out like it should be marking time, marking life. She stepped back, away from its reach, as it continued to pour out, pressing her further and further until it carpeted the concrete in a thin layer of building waste. Pressed against the wall, she watched it retreat to a trickle, then stop.

Ben knelt down on the floor, leaned forward, and dragged his hands through the dirt, swirling together the reds and whites until his skin was smeared with colours like a child fingerpainting. Cupping up larger chunks of rubble, he tipped his head back and licked his palms clean. Rachael heard the larger chunks grind against his toothless jaws.

"Stop now," she said, knowing how useless and pathetic it sounded, even before the words left her mouth.

He turned his head slowly, blood dripping from his chin into the mess by his knees.

"Stop now, get up and go and clean yourself up."

Something shifted behind his eyes, a switch turning a different way, a gateway closing and another opening, allowing in a different source of energy, but still he grasped handfuls of dirt and pressed it into his mouth, chewing and grinding with teeth no longer there.

Grabbing him by the neck, she forced open his mouth and scooped out the fragments of brick and mortar. Already his cheeks blistered from the lime, smooth and liquid against her hands. With most of the dirt scooped out, she dragged him backwards, across the room, far from the rubble. Reaching into her bag, she poured a bottle of mineral water over his face. The shock brought him back to realisation.

"What was that about?" she said, holding his shoulder so he couldn't stand. "What just happened?"

"I had no choice. It was from the other place, and if I don't make more then I won't be able to get back there."

The cough was more of a spasm in his chest. An eruption making him pitch forward away from Rachael's grasp. He landed on his hands and knees, face to the ground. The effort of holding himself in position was too great and he landed on his side.

The worms were not big, but there were many. They crawled over his empty and blistered jaws, wearing away the skin until they burst, then dragging the liquid with them. Rachael tried to turn away, but could not. They toppled over each other to get away from him, streaming over until they landed in the dirt and dust, their tails knotted together. Once on the floor, they shifted apart and retreated to the darkened corners of the room.

"What the fuck is going on?" she said. Ben still knelt on the concrete, forehead touching the floor. He stayed silent.

"We need to get you out of here," she said, trying to haul him back to his feet, but he did not move.

"They'll be coming now," he said. "They'll have heard the opening and they'll know that they can go behind the scenes to the cemetery of cities, where the nematodes of dirt find a path through skin and stomach. You've called them here."

"What are you talking about? You're having a breakdown. I know about the drinking. I knew when I took you on, but I thought the job might give you something to distract yourself. A focus."

He stood up, resting on Rachael for support, and pushed his finger between his lips, running a nail over the bleeding gaps.

"They're trying to find a way back. They'll be coming."

"I want you to get back to your hotel room. I want you to rest. I'll phone you a taxi."

"I can't leave," he said, his voice rising in pitch. "I can't go anywhere. We need to stay here. The backstage needs to be pure, and they won't keep it pure."

"Get up," she said, grabbing the front of his jacket and trying to haul him to his feet. Something around his legs severed with an audible break. For a moment she thought she had broken something. The worms erupting from his legs had drilled holes through his trousers. She looked at the ground below. Several holes pierced the concrete stained with white dust. Blood started seeping through the fabric. She dragged him across and leaned him against one of the compressors.

"That metal's nice and cool," he said, slumping backwards.

The knocking was loud and insistent. Rachael glanced back at Ben, rifled in her bag for her torch, and walked across to the door.

Chapter 15
Not By the Hairs

The two bolts slid home and she slumped against the locked door.

"Who is it?" she said. Across the room, Ben rested back against the compressor, tracing the metal as if it hid words only he could see.

"It's Peter. Herr Bettlemein's employee. He wants an update but can't get in touch with you on your handy. There's probably not much of a signal down here."

Rachael glanced at her phone screen, the signal bars at full power. She clicked through to the list of missed calls.

"No one's tried to contact me."

"Like I said, you'll not get a signal down here."

"Perfect connection, Peter. Nothing wrong with my phone."

"Well, he couldn't get hold of you and wants me to come in and speak to you in person."

"Okay, hang on a second."

There was a pause on the other side of the door.

"What are you doing?"

"I'm going to ring him. I'd rather speak to your boss in person."

There was a pause, and the knocking resumed twice as violent.

"Open this door. You don't need to speak to him. I'm his representative."

"I don't think so," she said. The phone took a moment to connect.

"Herr Bettelmein's office."

"Can you put me through to Herr Bettelmein, please?"

"I'm afraid he's taking his lunch at the moment. I can take a message."

"Tell him it's Frau Rachael Jenson. Tell him I have news for him."

On the other side of the metal, the knocking increased in violence.

"Open this fucking door."

"Frau Jenson. I hope everything is okay."

"Fine," she said, walking away from the hammering. "I've just had a missed call from Peter, and wanted to check whether there was a problem."

"I'm not sure why. I needed to assign Peter to another job today, across the city. I am happy to rely on your reports. Anything you need to tell me?"

"Nothing at all. Just making steady progress with the recording before we start the search for the rest of your documents."

"I understand that you need to be thorough. Please remember that I am funding your work for a reason."

"As if you would let me forget," she said. "I'll report to you at the end of the day."

She killed the call and glanced over at Ben. She had seen him in many stupors over the years, but this was the worst. Slumped to one side, drool staining his shirt. The pool of blood was no longer spreading from the leg wounds, soaked up by the pile of rubble.

"Open this door. Open it now. Let me in. I need to get in."

"I don't think I'll be doing that," she said. "I don't like liars."

"He was wrong. Whatever he told you was wrong. You know why he employs me, don't you? It's not to spy, it's to hurt people."

Rachael switched off. In great detail, he described what he would do to her and what he would do to Ben. Not the first time she had been threatened, she ignored him, though the knowledge that he meant every word sent her adrenaline coursing. Why hadn't she just told Herr Bettelmein about his rogue employee? Because then she'd have to explain about Ben and the building rubble and the worms, and she wasn't ready for that.

The worms. She only noticed them making their way across the room by the trails of Ben's spit and blood they left upon the floor. Now she watched them progress, she saw they were granular rather than fibrous. As they dragged themselves through the dirt, new fragments adhered to them, growing them in length. She stepped back to avoid their progress and watched them shuffle under the steel of the door.

The first thing that happened was Peter stopped speaking. The second was he started screaming. A number of the creatures passed through the steel of the door at head level, dropping to crumble back to dust on the floor. Then the third thing happened. A single gunshot, the bullet hitting the steel panels of the door.

"There'll be more, you know. He's only the first."

Ben was standing, leaning against the compressor, his mouth torn and bloody.

"What do we do?" It was a genuine question. If more people arrived as determined as Peter was, then it would not take them long to overwhelm the door.

"We go where they want to go and we seal up the exit behind us."

"And where is that?"

"We need to go backstage, into the Crawl Space."

"What do you mean Crawl Space?"

He pointed to the pile of brick dust on the floor.

"Where do you think this comes from?"

"Some hidden cavity?"

"In a manner of speaking," he said, smiling. His voice sounded more normal.

"How do we get there?"

He reached into a pocket and tumbled a pile of teeth into the middle of the floor. She watched them land on the dirt.

"You did it to yourself."

"It's the only way to get back there. Gift all of them and you can travel to and fro. The nematodes carry on living there. Recognise you. Do what you ask."

"Why all of them? Why did you do that to yourself?"

"Because once I found the capsules, I knew that I could get back, and if I gift all my enamel then I can go back and forth as much as I want."

"So we can get into this backstage place?"

He shook his head.

"I can. You need to pay a tithe to get there."

"A tithe?"

He fumbled in his pocket. She watched the nematodes of brick dust and cement crawl back across the floor to nest around his feet. They writhed and knotted, then crawled up him and back into his mouth.

"Just one, but you have to do it yourself. It has to be voluntary. I can't prise it from your face."

He held out the pliers and waited.

Chapter 16
Wrench

They were old, their metal handles wrapped with grey rippled duct tape, the tails of stick-like sigils just visible where the makeshift grips ended.

"They're going to scent that we've opened a path. The air from the Crawl Space tastes different, and they become attuned to it, and there will be many of them."

She took the pliers. The metal was warm, as if stored next to muscle and vein. They were not medical implements, but DIY tools. The type of thing used to extract words from the reluctant in dusty buildings in deniable places.

"Once you start, it doesn't hurt as much as you think, but we have to be quick. Give the path time to shed itself." When he spoke, it was as if a choir mouthed the words across his tongue. She knew that the worms were his clarity and she shuddered at the thought.

Elsewhere in the building she heard voices. Footsteps on the floor above. They were not quiet or patient. They had not yet found the door, but they would, and from the descriptions Peter had spat at her, she knew they would not stop until they entered and she was so much dust on the floor.

"Does it have to be a healthy tooth?" she said, leaning against the wall to steady herself while she spoke.

"It doesn't have to be a tooth at all. It can be a finger bone, or a fragment of skull. A vertebra or kneecap. Teeth are the easiest to remove. To answer your question though, no, it doesn't have to be healthy. Choose one near the front. They're easier to reach."

The incisor had turned grey from the inside out many years before. It gave her no pain and just shadowed her smile when the light was wrong.

The pliers were almost too big to fit in her mouth. Her tongue brushed the metallic jaws and she flinched at the taste and texture.

"Once you've got the pliers in place, rock the tooth back and forth until it feels loose, but please be quick."

There was no sensation when she tightened the handles, the pliers finally in place, no feeling in the enamel or the jaws. The dentist had told her long ago that the root was dead, just before she moved when she lost her job and couldn't find a new dentist. Her face could rot like her career as far as the wider world was concerned.

She felt the tooth start to move back and forth against the bone and soft tissue, and tasted blood in her mouth. With each compression, pain erupted through her mouth. Outside the door there were more voices; the sensation of the pliers stretching her cheeks as she writhed blocked out what they were saying, but there was no mistaking the tone. She could picture them pushing wet fingers into the holes the worms had left in Peter's body as they'd forced their way through his skin.

"Spit the blood out into the brick powder. Don't let it choke you."

She moved the pliers out and did as Ben said, watching the half-formed clot land damp and gelatinous in the dust.

The worms started as strands of blood, thickened with the small pieces of flesh from her gum. She watched them stretch through the dust, rolling around until they thickened to the size of her finger. Plaster dust. Wood splinters. Shards of glass. Outside fists were banging on the door, knuckles wet and scabbed.

"You need to speed up. If they get through the door then they can just ride the path behind us, and we won't be able to stop them. Try and keep the tooth whole, but if it cracks it cracks. The nematodes will fix it."

Rachael flinched at the thought of them crawling around inside her mouth, grazing her tongue and absorbing her words. She levered back and forth. Loosening and loosening. The words from outside were increasing in volume and number. They were working together to try and prise their way in. She gave a final wrench, and the infected incisor came loose, pain spreading like mycelium through her skull and shoulders.

"Give it to me," Ben said. The pain intensified as she tried to focus on his hand. Something crawled across her foot and settled around her ankle. She dropped the tooth into his palm and slumped to the floor.

Sight returning, she watched him drop the tooth into one of the capsules. Without asking, she knew it was an oversized one.

"Once they found out we had these, then they knew the path could be opened," he said. Vision clearing to a smear, she watched him walk around turning on the compressors. "But until we found this place, they didn't have the volume, and they still need to work together. They don't like that."

He rattled several objects into the capsule. She did not need to see them to know what they were.

"I need you focussed now," he said, with several echoes of the words overlapping with his. "When this has gone, we need to open every single cover and valve."

"Then what?" Her words felt wrong and sent scalpels of pain across her tongue.

"Then stand back and wait."

Chapter 17
Eruption

The pressure in the tubes built and she watched him walk over, open the oval glass panel, and slide the capsule inside.

The sound was from the future. A sound of Gernsback travel and stainless steel. A noise that promised cooperation and technology were the way to move across the world and beyond it.

"Now help me. We haven't got much time."

There were many tubes in the room, and many panels, and each needed to be unlocked by hand. Bolts loosened and latches unhooked. She felt Ben glancing over and turned, spitting a mouthful of blood clear. He nodded approval and she carried on, working as fast as her hands would let her. The pain now stretched down her arms and knitted across her fingers, but though she fumbled, each one came loose.

"We're nearly there. Last couple," Ben said. She looked at the bank of pipes before her and worked systematically down until she was crouched on the floor. A spasm of pain rocked her back on her heels.

"Now get back."

It began with a trickle. A slight dusting as if someone had tipped sweepings down the pipe and the last of the vacuum forced them out into the room. There was no sound beyond the compressors, then a grinding. A skittering. A pressure forcing air back into the room.

Brick dust came first. Fine and red. Coarse with shatters of mortar attached.

"Shelter behind something," Ben said, grabbing her arm. She winced as if every nerve in her body was attached to that single wrenched-free tooth. She felt the gap clotting now. Settling down. Her breath no longer finding its way into the bare bone of her jaw.

She recognised things in the rubble. Window frames and door hinges. Shattered light fittings. The broken porcelain of sinks and toilets, and over everything a fine choking cement dust that coated her skin and hair and eyes.

"Breathe it in," Ben said, though his voice sounded clogged. "I know it feels wrong, but you need to let the Crawl Space into your lungs before it will let you in."

From above her tumbled small broken sheets of plasterboard and floated fibreglass, catching in her hair and scratching her neck to ribbons.

Then the torrent started. She tried to scramble back out of the way, get to a place where she was safe, but the rubble came too fast. Broken laths, powdered breezeblocks, the force of their appearance pushing out clouds of expanded foam and polystyrene before them, and covering everything with a thick dust of plaster, concrete, and brick.

Larger fragments bounced off her limbs, bruising her skin. She glanced toward the door. Already the torrent was pressing against the metal, holding back the people outside. She could hear them now. They had some kind of grinder, trying to cut through the door.

"Is Bettelmein behind this?" she said to the room in general, but Ben in particular.

"Now's not the time. It's going to get worse in here before it gets better."

The pipes were all hidden now. Obscured behind the piles of rubble. Above her the ceiling was joists, the pipes no longer visible. They were compressing, coming closer and pushing the piles of rubble over to sweep down and cover what was already on the floor. She ducked, then lay flat, the dirt grinding into her skin. Ben was beside her, reaching out to grab her hand. His face was marked like body paint. Swirls of plaster and clay around his eyes and mouth. Arms streaked with cement.

"Close your eyes," he said. She did as he asked, ignoring the particles of dust scratching across her pupils. The joists were pushing on her back now, driving her deeper and deeper into the rubble and glass and splinters, until she was buried, the dust clogging her mouth and taking her breath. She had dug many graves in her career, and still she screamed, though the sound did not leave her lips, her lungs filling with dirt. Her breath went, then her feeling of touch, and then there was nothing.

Chapter 18
The Crawl Space

"Wake up." Ben was shaking her. Rachael opened her eyes and tried to focus. She coughed a long stream of dust and phlegm into the dirt and tried to turn over. She was lying on her back in a pile of fine dust. Around her, nematodes crawled through the mess and over her limbs. The floor above was no longer pressing her into the ground, but would still not let her stand.

"Don't move yet. Let your body get used to being here."

Ben was beside her. When he spoke, she saw he had teeth once more, but they were dirty white and red and granular. She reached inside her own mouth. The gap was no longer there, though the tooth was not smooth.

"The Crawl Space is generous, but can only work with the material it has."

She sat up, shuffling to shape the powder around her into a seat. There were other things in the dirt. Knuckle bones and femurs, tendons still attached, loose and wet. Discs of skulls, and at least half a jawbone. She picked it up and turned it over in her hand.

"Some people get desperate. They don't need to."

"What is this?"

"It's the Crawl Space. The gap between. The space to pass through. It's not easy to get into, but once you are, you can get almost anywhere."

Where his arms were bare, his skin was covered with dozens of wavering nematodes. Some were made purely of dust. Others were cruder and coarser, splinters of glass and silicon sealant wrapped around them. She reached out to touch them and they shrunk away into his skin.

"They're not very sociable. If we're going to spend some time here, you'll need to grow your own. They only really respond to their maker."

"To their maker?"

"They're made from your spit or blood, and the stuff of this place. They bind you here. The ones you made outside are okay, but when you make the nematodes here, they can guide you back."

She sat up and stared at him.

"Who the fuck are you?"

"I'm Ben. The same Ben you've worked with all those years."

"What is all this?"

"You remember when you went off digging around the country, after we finished on the M56 excavations?"

She nodded. She remembered it well. Six months of twelve-hour days, six days a week, then back to doing watching briefs in a field on the edge of No-One-Cum-Visitin' in Ruralwastelandshire.

"I got work doing building surveys. Recording old churches and barns. Private surveys for people with large houses and too much money."

"You never kept in touch."

He smiled, his rubble teeth flexing and shifting.

"I fell into a bottle a lot of the time. Then one day I was surveying this old detached place in the middle of a housing estate. We had to get underneath the floors to record the condition of some old timbers. They were reused and we could see the mortis hole above the floor. 13th century ship timber. I got the job of going down under the floor. There were traces."

Rachael picked up a handful of dirt and let it fall through her fingers like time. She looked around for something she could use as a weapon. The largest object was the fragment of jawbone, and even that felt like rot-softened wood.

"So I'm crawling under this floor, and the dirt. The dirt isn't part of the construction. The dirt is something else. There are things moving in it. I flinch away, but there's nowhere to move. And I find myself pressed down into here. I don't know why or how I got here without the sacrifice, but I did."

"So you had a hallucination, probably brought on by lack of oxygen or a gas leak, or some other such thing."

"Does this look like a hallucination? And once I had these attached to me," he said, picking up one of the nematodes and watching it break in half. "Then I knew I had to get back."

He sat up and looked around him.

"We need to move. Just in case they work out how to get here."

She looked around again for a weapon, sifting and digging down through the dust to find a shard of glass, or a fragment of porcelain. Her search was interrupted by Ben's laughter.

"It doesn't work like that here. The only weapons are those which you make." Several of the worms tipped out of his mouth and lost themselves around his feet.

"Can you get us back?"

"Why would you want to go back? There's everything here. This dirt, this rubble around your feet, connects you to everything. The forts along Hadrian's Wall, Salisbury Cathedral. The Library of Alexandria. All of it ends up here. Dust and dirt and splinters and fragments."

"And what's above us?" Rachael said, running her hand over the wood of the joists barely three feet above her head.

"We need to get going now. If they catch us before we can prepare, then we don't stand a chance."

"I thought you said that they wouldn't be able to follow."

"It takes a large sacrifice to open a path like the one we took. There are a lot of them. They've been gathering for weeks, and there will be one who will do what is needed. We need to get to a safe place. Somewhere we can defend."

Chapter 19
Duck and Cover

The ground dropped away and they dropped with it, sliding over the shattered breezeblocks and iron reinforcement bars that snagged their clothes. Occasionally the rusted metal grazed Rachael's skin. From somewhere inside her arm, the worms filled the wound, squirming around in the loose blood that collected in the cut until there was nothing but twitching where the wounds had been. She gagged and closed her eyes.

"We need to keep moving," Ben said. "Keep moving down. If we can get to the Valley of Feathers, we might be able to distract them. Put them off the scent."

From above, Rachael heard voices. A vast tumble of syllables crashing against each other making no coherent sense, as if the words themselves were rubble tumbling away from demolition.

"How far do we have to go?"

Ben paused and turned. She tried not to look at his teeth as he spoke. Tried not to imagine the same in her own mouth.

"The Crawl Space shifts and moves. There's no consistency. Just the centre and everything else."

"So there isn't a Valley of Feathers, then?" she said.

"The geography is permanent, but not fixed."

They continued sliding downhill, over a tumble of shattered porcelain.

"Of course geography is fixed, otherwise it's not geography."

"Not here."

"So how do you get anywhere?"

Rachael rested her hand on a shatter of white pottery, the surface obscured with crusted yellow mineral.

She wasn't squeamish. She'd dug bodies out of the ground for years, both wet and dry. Sat in vans with skulls of the dead resting on plastic trays in her lap. Ladled corpse juice out of a coffin into a container, watching the artificial teeth floating around in the sludge. She wasn't squeamish, and yet the texture of crusted piss still turned her stomach.

"You're going to have to get used to it," Ben said, taking her arm and moving her farther down the slope. "At least part of the tooth replacing your sacrifice."

She vomited. There was no way to stop it. It was a completely automatic response. The liquid hit the ground and coalesced into a nest of nematodes that separated from each other. Loosened, they crawled across the dirt and soil, grasping for her, gripping her shoes and pulling themselves against her skin.

"I'm really not up for this," Rachael said, trying to brush them away. "Really not up for this at all."

"They're here to help you. Just go with it for now."

"And if I don't? If I hang back, or wait for those coming behind?"

"Then they will hollow you out and fill you with nematodes of their own making, then a bit of dried urine will be the least of your worries."

He turned his back and ignored her. She raged under her breath. Raged that she was trapped in this world of decay and desecration. Dirt and destruction. Nothing was together.

"You were asking how you find anything in a place with no fixed points."

She did not answer.

He shrugged.

"Like this."

Rachael watched him lift his arms. The nematodes swirled up into the air, dragging strands of corrugated sheeting and steel reinforcement after them. Ben stared down at his feet, eyes closed. With one hand he reached through the whirl of rubbish around him. Rachael could barely see him anymore. Fractures and splinters sliced open his skin, blood pooling in the crooks of his arms. He leaned down to lick the wounds, then started to chant. Around her, the world shifted. The air tasted of dust and dirt, then something else. Something more organic. A tickle against her tongue. Something hollow and brittle snapping between her teeth. She tried to steady herself, find her feet, but fell face-first, bracing herself for the impact on sherds of sharp brick.

The landing was soft and cushioned, if slightly scratchy. Rachael sat up and tried to heave a lungful of air into her system.

"Where are we?"

"The Valley of Feathers."

Chapter 20
The Valley of Feathers

The valley they sat in was indeed covered in feathers, but most of them were attached to rotting meat and shattered bone. As far as the eye could see there was nothing but dead pigeons. Some were little more than wings or skulls, others clumps of torsos, coated with tattered down.

"They have a special affinity with buildings," Ben said, giving her an explanation she didn't ask for or particularly want. "No one quite knows why, but when they die in the lofts of old buildings, the Crawl Space seems to consider them part of the fabric."

"But not enough of a building material, so they end up here?"

"No one knows why that happens either. Stay there, and whatever happens next, don't move."

The squawking was the first thing she noticed. That, and then the shuffling underneath where she lay. The sound of feathers scraping against each other. Bones detaching themselves from the ground. Lifting themselves away. She scrabbled to find somewhere safe and glanced up. High above her head she could still see the unvarnished wood of the floor from underneath. The birds were alive. Or not alive, but moving. Ben stood dragging nematodes from his skin, draping each one into the mass of decaying birds. Letting them eat them where they had beaks or sliding them under the feathers where they didn't. Soon the creatures were crowding him, like flocks at feeding time. Several crawled over Rachael to get to the treats, one wearing a racing ankle tag.

"You need to make some too. I won't be able to control them all."

"Make some?"

"Use the worms. It's what they are for."

She reached under her trouser leg and felt them squirm as she tried to grab hold of them.

"Calm down. If you're calm, they're calm. You're shooting them through with adrenaline at the moment. Take a moment. Still yourself."

"Have you looked around?" she said to herself, but too loud.

"And the only way we're going to get anywhere is if we work together. Stay calm. Feed the nematodes to the dead birds, and then we'll be ready to cover our tracks."

He said it with the calm of a practised professional. Like he was delivering a medical diagnosis or recommending a wine to accompany a meal.

Holding the first nematode, she reached out for a pigeon, catching something that was barely more than a pair of wings and a rib cage. With shaking hands, she fed the nematode into the gap where the head should be and waited.

"Don't just do one. We need a flock."

Over and over again she grasped rotting feathers and mould-stained bone, trying not to flinch when the desiccated skin brushed her hand. Time and time again she fed the partial birds nematodes torn from her limbs. She watched Ben doing the same, completely at ease with the devastation around them. Not flinching or nervous, just focussed.

In the distance was a grinding sound. Like teeth crumbling in unsettled sleep. A buzzing erosion getting closer.

"They'll be here soon," Ben said, stepping over the worm-fed corpses. "How many have you made?"

Rachael looked around her feet.

"About thirty. Will that be enough?"

"I've got about sixty. It's a good start," he said. "Stand up."

She stood, being careful not to crush any of the birds around her feet.

"Now I need you to partition off your brain. It sounds wrong, but it will come easier. There's part of your brain which belongs to you. The part that makes you move and makes decisions. Then there is a second part. That belongs to the Crawl Space. You need to partition that part off. Let it set on its own."

Rachael was used to partitioning. Partitioning off work from home. Family from the rest of her life. The disappointment of those around her from her need to actually do something rather than wallow.

She felt around in her thoughts for an idea that wasn't hers. She wasn't sure what she was looking for, but it was a scent. The scent of soil freshly dug from the ground, stained with petrol. It was a smell that had always turned her stomach, but this thought revelled in it. Wanted to smear it across the floor and bathe in it. She held the idea, stretched it out.

Wound it together like cotton around a reel, then, slowly but surely, set up a wall in her head.

"With that side of your thoughts you can control the birds," Ben said, reaching out to put a reassuring hand on her shoulder. She flinched.

She wasn't a touchy person anyway. Hated being hugged. Hated being affectionate with friends. But this was something more. She felt something under his skin. This place. Whatever else he was, however much he was Ben, he was a creature of this place. The Crawl Space. There was something embedded within him that would not go. And something embedded within her recognised that. She was flinching at herself, not him.

She tasted the feathers in her mouth. Felt the bones stretch from her fingers like twigs from a vase. There was a moment when she felt herself flex and twist, worm-like and segmented. With two hands she stretched out her palms and pressed them against the dust-filled air. With a shudder of feather scales, the birds took to the air in all their decay and rose higher and higher until they reached the floor above them. She smelled the varnish that had dripped between the floorboards and the sawdust that stuck to the rough-sawn timber with dried blood, and she held her pets there. Her other selves. She held them there and waited.

Chapter 21
Many-Limbed and Crawling

The noise was the sound of grinding. Grinding of metal against concrete. Teeth that tore and splintered. The sound of metal against flesh and skin. The screams that came with it. She glanced up to the ridge.

The Calthemites were torn open. Rib cages and mouths rammed full of cement and glass. The noise they made was halfway between song and scream, vocal cords cut and split. There were words too. Implications. Threats.

She flinched as Ben covered her ears. Moving his fingers, he whispered.

"Turn away. Nothing good can come from seeing them."

But it was too late. The Sacrifice had been gifted a new body of metal, reinforced concrete and shattered brick. When it walked, the chips fell loose to swirl around its feet, then return to his body and embed themselves once more in the exposed muscles that bled and wept copper-stained water to the floor.

"You need to focus on the birds. Hold my hand, and when you feel me shift my flock, you do the same."

His skin on hers meant something other than revulsion. The Crawl Space that lurked within them both found each other. Bridged between. Used their nerves and skin for its own needs. They were unimportant. Conduit. Pipework.

The birds swooped down from high in the gloom. Many-feathered and splinter-boned, they dropped from the sky, flew around Ben and Rachael once, though many had no wings. Then curved down toward the mass of Calthemites.

Somewhere inside, Rachael felt the now razor-sharp feathers sever the Calthemites into quarters. Felt the skin and bone fall to the ground. The Sacrifice flayed around to try and catch the wings and was in turn flayed, all the brittle bones of porcelain and glass exposed. As one, the flocks descended, as if every fragment was seed, and tore it apart. Each one carried away a beak full of dust, of cement, of splinters that they sprayed far away. A rain of a second death that coated skin and rubble alike.

Rachael was so busy concentrating on what she was doing that she barely noticed the shift beneath her. The wings shuddering. New birds rebirthing from the charnel that lay underfoot.

"They're organising," Ben said. "They've got enough focus to move their own birds into the air."

"But they haven't implanted nematodes. How can they do that?"

"We're using magic. They're using prayer. They worship this place. It is their god. We need to go."

The dead pigeons underfoot were not flying, instead shifting to one side. Moving away. Leaving holes and hollows. Rachael tried to find solid footing. Somewhere to walk. Somewhere to push herself free. There was nowhere. She was falling, and then the dead were covering her over and her mouth was filling with feathers and she was dying, choking on the splinters of the dead.

Chapter 22
The Sea is Not Made of Water

She was underground. The weight of tons pressed down on her limbs and her lungs. Held her in place. Somewhere to one side, not sure if it was right or left, there was the sound of movement, swimming, though she was not in water. Her lungs felt full of dust and her mouth of mould. She waited. Stretched out her arms and grabbed whatever was passing her.

Ben slid one of his nematodes from his skin and fed it to her. She flinched as the creature slid across her tongue, then turned back to powder, staining her teeth and throat. Without waiting to ask her, he tore free one of hers and pressed it between his own lips.

"I'm sorry. I needed to do that. There's no way to speak here without drowning again, and if we drown again then we may not get to the surface."

The voice was in her chest. A pressure against her diaphragm.

"Will I always be able to hear you? Even when I don't want to?"

"I'm sorry," he said. She tasted the words as wet paper and salt. "You need to follow me now. We need to get to shore."

She watched him disappear through the waves of dead corpses, sweeping them out of the way with vast strokes, like he was dragging himself against a particularly strong current. She followed, trying to ignore the scrape of beaks against her skin, and in their clutching she heard the sound of that skull-tremoring song. The decay and death in those non-words. The birds knew that song as well. She needed to swim away from it. The nematodes scavenged from the dead to keep themselves in one piece. She let them help her drag herself away through the corpses that stained her skin with their feathered rot.

"Keep going. We don't have far to go now." The sensation of the words made her gag. He was inside her and there was no way to untangle him from her bones.

Under her feet, under the feet of dead birds, she felt solid land. Pressing down, she forced her head up through the wings and feathers, taking a large intake of breath. The floor was closer above them now, and the air was filled with the scent of old wet paper.

Chapter 23
The Word Can Rot as Well as Anything

She picked up the nearest book, a cheap paperback, the cover separating. Holding it high, she watched the pages flutter free to land across her lap. The nematodes gnawed at the edges like caterpillars unfettered in an allotment.

Books covered the ground in every direction. Some were nested in cardboard boxes, but most were just scattered and abandoned, swollen and forgotten. She searched around for Ben, but there was no sign, and the voice in her chest was silent.

Reading had always been a big part of her life. She remembered playing in her grandparents' garden and finding the stack of old boxes in the shed. Row upon row of forgotten paperbacks. Secret Service spies, and bikers with American words that sounded trite in their English mouths. The covers were torn and spotted with mould, but she could hide there and read them whenever the choice took her, the scent of lilac and magnolia on the air.

There was no lilac now, or magnolia. Just the scent of damp that clung to her clothes. She scrabbled over the stack of rotting paper and tried to keep her balance. Her feet slipped from underneath her and she landed face-first in a pile of *Reader's Digest* abridged editions that scuttled away from her. She grasped a nearby book and turned over the cover. The words were mildew-blurred, barely visible, never mind legible. She arced it through the air, watching it land and the nearby stack of amateur sleuth knockoffs stumble away.

"We can use them," a voice inside said. She turned. Ben crouched nearby, arms around his legs. His face was covered with short lengths of reinforcement bar that twitched and shrank as he spoke.

She lifted one of the books high in the air, watching the pages slide away from the spine. Picking one up, she tried to read the first sentence.

"This doesn't make any sense. There are no coherent words in these old books. They're just rubbish."

Ben took the page from her.

"Nothing is rubbish here, because everything is rubbish. Nothing is useless because everything is useless. This is where all the destruction comes. All the waste. Pass me a page."

She did as he asked, handing him a handful of paper. Dropping all but one, he began reading. The words swirled and danced in the air, became solid, and burrowed down into the rest of the mass of pulp, dragging out stacks and volumes.

"These are not just abandoned books, but contain the magic of the Crawl Space. They're grimoires and books of shadows." He handed one over.

"This is nothing. There is nothing of worth here. Nothing to read or speak."

"That's because you're reading it wrong. You're seeing the words as flat on the paper. You need to see the paper as a block. Look through the block."

She held the paper up to the gloom. There was no light source to glow through the sheets.

"Use the nematodes."

She felt them detach. Crawl away from her skin and anchor themselves onto the paper. Where they had left dents in her skin, she felt the texture of paper against her muscle. With a shimmer, the nematodes began to burrow through the book. The words bloomed in her head like pinprick flowers, petals of sounds unfurling. She felt her bones shift, reorganise to let the words come out of her mouth. Across the mountain of books, Ben ran from something she couldn't see. She let the words fade and he calmed, pausing and catching his breath.

"See what I mean? It's easy."

Her voice still didn't return to herself. Placing her hands upon her waist, she coughed, and continued coughing. Letting everything held in her stomach rise out in a spume of spit and dust. Evacuated every part of the Crawl Space that was in her. Let her own voice find its way back.

"I will not speak through some kind of mediation, and I will not let this place become part of me."

Ben shook his head. It was hard now to tell where the nematodes ended and he started. He was fronded and fringed, a blur of movement.

"You won't survive."

"Then I won't survive. I will not become of this place."

"You need to be careful, Rachael. The Crawl Space listens."

"The Crawl Space listens. The Crawl Space speaks. You talk about the Crawl Space like it's a living thing, and all it is is waste. It's a dumping ground for all the rubbish and rubble the world cannot hold anymore."

He reached out to place his hand on hers.

"You do not fucking touch me. You get me out of here."

"I can't do that. We're too far from an entrance, and it would take too long to go back. The Calthemites are there. We would not be able to get past them."

She did not notice the vibrating at first, the sensation so unusual and so unexpected. Mechanical and not organic.

She reached into her pocket and pulled out her phone.

"Hello?" Her own voice sounded unfamiliar.

"Frau Jenson. What do you have to tell me?"

Chapter 24
Call Waiting

"Herr Bettelmein. How did you get hold of me so easily?"

"I phoned the number you provided. I do hope you have an update for me. I hate to waste money on dead ends."

"Of course. I understand that money is your first priority. We've hit a bit of an impasse. It's going to take us some time to get back on track. I know that patience isn't your greatest attribute, but please just bear with us until I contact you again."

"You are right that patience is something I don't normally indulge in. I hope that I haven't made a mistake in assigning this project to you."

"Of course not, Herr Bettelmein. You don't have many options anyway. There is no one else that can do this work for you. No one else has my expertise."

"And your colleague? I hope he isn't distracting you too much from the task in hand."

"Ben? Ben is an asset in all my undertakings."

"Ben, as you refer to him, is a borderline alcoholic with a diseased liver and failing kidneys."

"His medical issues and personal life are no concern of mine."

"Nor mine, until they prevent you finishing this contract."

The phone was wrenched from her hand and she watched it arc across to land on a pile of old rotten magazines.

"What the fuck did you do that for?"

"Look," Ben said. "Just look."

Chapter 25
The Verdigris Cord

Trailing from the top of the handset was a single thin strand of corroded copper, made up of fragments of stained water pipes and short lengths of electrical wiring. The phone skittered across the fans of book pages for a moment and returned to her hand. She lifted it to her head.

"Supposition. Drowning. Cantaloupes, and suicide in a brown villa on the moor. Sleeping with the dead under a bunk bed where fish explode toward the moon."

"Let me have a listen," said Ben, leaning in so close his nematodes recoiled from her. "If you were ever talking to Bettelmein, you're not now. That's something that's trying to replicate a conversation. Have you ever been fishing?"

Rachael shook her head.

"That's a lure. A trap to drag in the prey. You're the prey."

The phone wrenched, dragging her across the dampened pages. Several of the covers stood proud of the mess of pulp and sliced papercuts into her arms and legs. She winced, and tried to dislodge the phone from her grip, but it wouldn't leave. She glanced up.

The Calthemites were gathered on the edge of the plain of books, the Sacrifice at the front. From its mouth, a line of copper trailed like a strand of spit, leading across the water-rotten cheap paperbacks to her hand. As she watched, it chewed the copper back into itself with teeth of safety glass, dragging her closer and closer.

She could not stand and she could not remove the phone. Around the Sacrifice, the Calthemites chanted words she did not understand. She recognised several of them. Peter, his face deformed by a nest of scars and plasterboard parasites. Beside him, the woman who had pulled her tooth out to show Rachael. Her eyes were faceted with window glass, pulsing in and out as if the words she chanted dragged air from inside her skull. She knew she could not let herself be captured by them.

Grasping with her one free hand, she tried to hold one to the ground, but her fingers either slid off the dampened spines or pushed through the saddened paper. The pace of the recoil increased, dragging her on. She stumbled, losing her footing. Somewhere in the distance she could hear Ben shouting advice to her, but the chanting had gotten louder and robbed her of any other sound. She tried to pivot to see him, but he was too far now. She was on her own. Turning again, she fell and tried to concentrate on his shouting. Only one word came through.

"Nematodes."

The place in her head was damp and stained, decorated with mildewed wallpaper and rotting sofas. She nestled in there and found the pipe that led out to the rest of her body. To the worms that nestled upon her skin. They understood her words.

Opening her eyes, she felt them crawl up her throat and erupt from her mouth like a burst infection, crawling down her arm toward the phone.

She felt herself within them and she felt the Crawl Space in there too. A constant craving to drag the broken and damaged to itself. Not to repair it or to fix it, but to give it a home, and a place to be broken and damaged on its own terms. She watched the nematodes shift themselves into the phone, the speaker exploding in static as they did so. She did not belong here. She was not damaged or broken or forgotten. This was not her home. She did not need this home. The verdigris tether bulged and deformed as the creatures that were her and not her forced their way into it. Disrupted the signal coming from the Sacrifice. In her hand, the phone fell away from her palm and smashed on the floor, and as it tarnished and fractured in front of her eyes, she flinched. Would that happen to her too? A falling away and a separating. The nematodes were closer now, but the Calthemites had not seemed to notice, so focussed on their chants and devotionals. As the creatures pressed on, the line behind fell away, spattering the novels below with green stains that burnt holes into the pages. The nematodes reached the jaws of the Sacrifice and crawled in.

The screaming was uncontrolled and unending, and then she realised that it was coming from inside her too. The nematodes were showing her how they sacrificed the creature in front of her, and how it now saw the world, and she felt its pain and sorrow and the ending nature of its agony, and knew there was no way to ease that torment.

Something tightened around her wrist, and for a moment she thought that the Sacrifice's glass teeth were grinding through her bone.

"We need to run, and we need to run now." Ben's face was stained with sweat and ash, the iron bars falling away like loose eyelashes.

"Where can we run so that they won't catch us? They're as much a part of this place as we are. They'll just keep chasing us."

"We just need to get somewhere to buy us some time and plan. Get enough ground between us so we can bed in and defend ourselves."

"Are there any buildings here at all? Anything we can hide within?"

"No, but we can build something. We need to get to the Hill of Damp Solidity."

"The what the fuck now?"

"You remember on building sites there would always be at least one bag of cement left to get wet in the rain?"

"Yes."

"And it would become a solid bag of absolutely no use?"

"The builders would call them bags of fuck all good."

Ben smiled, and she could see his tongue was coated with a slime of rainwater, teeming with tiny brick-chip beetles.

"Those end up here, and while they may be useless and abandoned in the outside world, in the Crawl Space, they can be used to build."

Chapter 26
The Hill of Damp Solidity

They walked, sometimes ducking as the roof lowered, sometimes stretching out. Other times crawling hand over hand, the broken fenceposts and shattered breezeblocks cutting their hands to ribbons. Behind them was a constant buzzing sound. The noise of the Calthemites in the distance. Always behind. Always coming.

The Hill of Damp Solidity was not a hill, but a mountain, a glacial spill of lump after lump of concrete, each one coated in tattered paper. Some of the symbols she recognised. The blue circle, the grey-capped bags, and the crimson dragon.

"We need to work now, before the Calthemites reach us."

"Work doing what?" she replied, watching several paper-wrapped boulders tipping down the slope to shatter open.

"We need to build defences. Build a wall that stretches across the pathway so they can't follow. They'll break it down eventually, but it will slow them."

Rachael looked around. She knew how much physical work was involved in tasks. How many barrow-loads it took to empty a ditch section of mattocked clay. How many shovel-loads to shift a spoil heap. She stared around at the vast open plain of rot and broken things, and listened to the distant scratching of their pursuers.

"It's too big a task," she said, not in fear, but in a point of realism. Something that tasted so unfamiliar at that moment.

"You're right," Ben said. "We need help."

"Don't tell me. The nematodes."

He shook his head and pointed to her hands.

"You need to scrape away the dead skin. As much as you can."

"What do you mean, scrape away the dead skin?"

"Run your nails across your neck and arms. Across your legs. Get as much dead skin into your nails as you can, then scrape it from there into your palm. Have I been wrong so far?"

And she had to allow that he hadn't. So far. So far, he'd kept her alive and out of the clutches of the Sacrifice. She watched him do the same. Run his dirt-encrusted fingernails across his cheeks and forehead. She echoed his movements.

A few minutes later, a pile of dead grey skin sat in the palm of her hand.

"What now?"

"Look," he said.

The skin cells were organising themselves into something else. She peered closer. A tiny figure lay against her skin, writhing in its newly discovered life. She held it up to the light.

"That's not going to be able to lift much."

"Wait," Ben said, and because she didn't know the rules and he seemed to, she waited.

Something brushed against her eyes, and she noticed streams of fine dust flying through the air toward her. The same happening to Ben. A typhoon of dirt focussing on his hand. She glanced down at her own and saw the homunculus had grown, now as long from fingertip to wrist. There was barely any weight as it sat on the edge of her palm and dropped to the ground. It did not stop growing, more swarms of muck coming through the air and enlarging the thing.

"What is going on?"

"You know what they say about skin making up so much of dust? It's true, and it all ends up here. The creature down there is made up of your dead skin cells, and like calls to like."

"But even with two helpers made of a web of dead skin, how's that going to help?"

"Patience."

A few moments later, the creation was the same size as Rachael, the edges blurred and transparent, and matching Rachael's own outline. It stepped away from her to the middle ground, and there split, and split again and again, each one more transparent. Faded figures with faded edges of dust. By the time they stopped, there were twenty-one replicas of Rachael and twenty-one replicas of Ben.

"Skin remembers," he said, followed by something in a dialect Rachael did not recognise, but guessed was the language of the Crawl Space itself. As the syllables settled into the air, the replicas began to lift the vast cement blocks, the weight of them not an issue for their faint and febrile limbs.

Rachael crouched and hooked her fingers under one of the fossilised sacks of manmade stone.

"What are you doing?" Ben said, reaching around the other side.

"Helping doing whatever we're doing. What are we doing?"

"You already are. The skin that makes up those? They're you. They're as much you as any of the cells that make up your body. And they don't get tired, and I need you to have as much energy as possible."

She nodded and sat down on a single frozen bag and watched. Working on their own, the creatures of dust each grabbed bags far beyond Rachael's ability to carry and then came together to build them into a vast wall. They worked fast. At times she thought that the dust making them up would separate, returning them to little more than a fine web of death coating the air, but no. They held together by some force she did not know nor care to know.

"Will this stop them?"

"Stop the Calthemites? Probably not. They have their own ways to make progress, as you've seen. The Sacrifice is their most powerful weapon here, but there are others."

"So what are they after? They aren't just pursuing us, are they? You don't just go searching for people. You don't sacrifice people to chase strangers. They're after something else. Something you're looking for too, I'm guessing."

"I'm helping you to survive. I kept you alive and got you here. They would have killed you. Turned you into the Sacrifice."

"Not willingly."

"There are ways to persuade."

By now the dust doppelgangers had built a wall several courses long that curved around at the flanks. Every time they lifted one of the bags of solid cement, Rachael felt a tug against her skin. Nothing more than a slight discomfort, like a thread had snagged somewhere out of sight.

"So you're telling me that you're not looking for something? You're just keeping me alive?"

Ben climbed up the wall and peered over the top.

"They'll be here soon. We need to leave."

"And them?" Rachael said, pointing to the faded figures still working below.

"They'll just blow away on the breeze."

Rachael lifted her arm up. There was no air moving at all. Everything was still. She turned once more to look at the defence and the creatures still constructing it, the slight nagging sensation with every lift, and then followed Ben up the slope.

"Wait," she said. He paused above her and turned. Rachael closed her eyes and concentrated. She entered the Crawl Space part of her brain and called to the dust doppelgangers to abandon their work. To follow her. She felt them resisting. There was no consciousness there. Just her will implanted in a shape that echoed hers. She found that kernel of thought and tore it apart. Let it fall to the ground and replaced it with one to follow her. Opening her eyes, she watched all twenty-one of them turn toward her and Ben, falling in step behind.

"They need to finish building the wall," Ben said, staring at her. She noticed his eyes were filled with flecks of rust and limescale, shifting constantly as if dancing in the light.

"If they're as close behind as you say, then it won't make a huge amount of difference, and yours can stay here to continue building. We may need help farther along."

She watched the fight for arguing go out of him. His shoulders slumped and hands came up.

"Leave four there, and bring the others."

Rachael looked behind her. The dust doppelgangers. Four peeled away to rejoin the working party.

"Thank you. We need to move now. Get as far as we can."

"Can we not bring the place to us?"

Ben shook his head.

"We've built something here now. We've created an anchor. Can't sail with an anchor."

"So we have to walk the rest?"

"We have to walk the rest," Ben agreed.

"And where are we walking to?"

"To our destination."

They set off in silence, the only way Rachael could hide her annoyance, her frustration at being stonewalled all the time by Ben. They had known each other a long time. Not always friends, but a long time. She did not expect him to treat her like this. To try and take advantage of her lack of knowledge or experience to pull rank. Behind them, the dust doppelgangers kept step with her. Echoed her movements, pale and faded.

Chapter 27
The Avenue of Pillars

The going was hard, the ground covered in larger lumps of concrete than they'd encountered so far. Every few metres they paused so that the dust doppelgangers could go first, fluttering up the sharp cliffs of demolished buildings so they could drag Ben and Rachael after.

He was hiding something, like a bottle of vodka in his jacket or the reek of whiskey on his breath. She knew he was good at concealing. Holding things back. She was better at spotting patterns, whether that was in the change of soils on a site, or the nervous glances to the left by someone who was hoping the litre of vodka in their coat wasn't clanging against something. The questions would have to wait until they got to a place of safety. Not that she knew what that looked like anymore. She ran her hand along the razored edge of a piece of rebar and stared at the rust stain on her fingers. The nematodes on her arms craned to try and reach the corrosion. She flinched and rubbed her hand on her trousers.

"I know where we are," said Ben, pointing away in the distance. "Or, I know where we'll be in a few minutes. The Avenue of Pillars."

She shrugged and started walking, the dust doppelgangers silently copying her movements. She did not want to sightsee. She wanted to get home.

The ground rose until they needed to crawl on their stomachs across a mass of broken roof tiles, the wooden floor above them scraping against her back. She winced and felt bruises erupt along her spine as she dragged herself along, hand by hand, over a lake of shattered terracotta.

Reaching the other side, she pivoted and sat next to Ben. He pointed down below them.

"The Avenue of Pillars."

The description was fitting. Running as far as the eye could see was a narrow path, flanked on both sides by broken columns of plaster, stone, and marble. She recognised Doric, Ionic, Romanesque shafts of golden stone, and small columns once belonging to some long-forgotten art gallery. All were stained or smashed or broken, but they stood in equality. Whether their bases were shattered or their terminals lost, they stood alongside each other. An honour guard for a walk no one was meant to make. She saw stripped-bark trees and bundled canes blackened by fire. All were positioned to respect each other and with no differentiation in value.

"Have you been here before?" she said, curiosity overriding any desire she had to try and keep up her defences.

"Once," he said. "I manifested down there once."

"And did you walk the path? Is it a way out? Is it an escape route?"

Ben leaned forward with his head in his hands and muttered something Rachael didn't quite catch. He turned toward her.

"There is no escape. There is no way out of here. If we leave, they'll pursue us in the real world, and there they'll capture us in moments. Here we stand a chance. We can use the Crawl Space against them. Come on. It shouldn't take us long to get down there, and you really need to see them up close."

They slid like children on a grass slope, letting gravity take their weight down toward the narrow path. At the bottom they stood in the shadows and waited for the dust doppelgangers to catch up.

The sensation started in Rachael's diaphragm, spreading out along her arms and legs like an infection. Less pain and more of a dragging sensation that felt like her skin was separating from her muscles. She winced and tried to hide her discomfort. Ben was doubled up, arms around his knees, gasping in lungfuls of air.

"It'll pass," he said, waving her away. "The Calthemites have gotten through the defences and consumed the doppelgangers. They'll know where we're going. We need to move. They'll be here soon."

"Are you okay to move?"

"In a minute. Give me a minute."

She wondered if it was more intense, his discomfort. She ignored the sensation and walked up to the nearest column, running her hand down the grooves to try and distract herself. It didn't work. The pain intensified. An erupting. A pressing out. She turned around.

The dust doppelgangers stood a short distance away. There was something changing, a solidity that was lacking before. She watched them shrink and lessen, the motes that made their shape getting closer and closer, then the air was filled with nothing but the sound of screaming.

The Calthemites each filled the space taken by the doppelgangers and stepped out between her and Ben, finally the Sacrifice clawing its way through. She felt them under her skin, as if they had just climbed out from under her own ribs. She knew she had to run, despite the pain, but could not drag herself away from watching what happened next.

Chapter 28
Alone Again

This was the first time she had seen the Calthemites up close. They all wore scars and nematodes extending several feet into the air. When they spoke, small eruptions of brick powder caught the air.

"We will eat him and then we will feed you to our Sacrifice and we will find the First Ruin." Their voices faded in and out as they choired the words.

She waited for Ben to say something. Give her some instructions. She stared at him. She had no clue what she was doing. Where she should go. How to run. She waited. She waited and he said nothing. Then he turned to stare at her.

"Please don't leave me."

They were on him dragging blades of glass out of their gullets, plunging them into his neck and peeling apart his skin, reaching their hands into his cracked bones. She braced herself for the gore; the grief she put off until later.

There was none. Instead of intestines and veins, they pulled dust and half-bricks from underneath his skin. Lengths of window frame, coving, and stair-rods.

Slowly, with teeth of plaster, they consumed him from within. The thing that had once been Peter leaned over Ben's face, scraping sharp nails of forgotten razors into his eyes and licking off the rust. There was nothing left to do but run.

Chapter 29
Beyond the Path

Beat expectations. That had been the message all the way along. Be better, faster, quicker than him, or him, or them. Because if she wasn't brighter, funnier, with a bigger capacity for alcohol, they would reduce her to some shadow. Empty her barrows for her. That's how they started. Reduce her. Reduce her work. She fucked them all off. They'd always start the same way. Offering to help her out. Tell her how to identify a context. Tell her how to fill out a context sheet. Take her barrow for her. Thing was, she could shovel three times as fast as they could empty them, so they'd rush to keep up. Only once did someone break their leg trying to match her pace. By the end of the day, she was digging her own section and emptying their barrows. Now she needed to defeat a different set of expectations.

They would think she was going to follow the path. Go between the pillars into the distance. A set vector. A steady division between the x and y. She needed to rise through the z. Throw them off completely. She took a breath and glanced behind her. They were still feasting on Ben, the Sacrifice striding around their cordon like a barely leashed beast. Ben's head kept talking as it twitched, a broken animatronic. She wondered if it was talking about her. Giving clues to her identity. Giving away how she thought. How she acted. She glanced back once more. Confound expectations, then exceed them. She stepped between the pillars, then stepped once more.

It was not an avenue, but a forest.

The pillars stretched far into the distance. They weren't just decorative or structural. There were fenceposts and marquee stakes. Circles of stockades damaged by gunfire, and concrete piles rising into the air, their surface pitted with gravel and soil.

She let herself become lost. There was no reason not to. She had no destination. No way to go that was proscribed. Ben's opaque words meant she had no direction, so she wandered. Let the next thought lead her onto a path of her own making.

The air was so still she could hear the Calthemites behind her. There was no doubt in her mind that they would catch her, especially as she was on her own and did not know the rules. Lost in a woodland of broken posts and shattered drainpipes. They could not get in track of her. There was no track to get in front of. Along her limbs, the nematodes twitched like coral. She held out her arm. All the tiny worms pointed straight up in the air, pencil-lined.

With no better plan, she took their lead and stopped in position. What were the Calthemites expecting her to do? They were expecting her to move. Expecting her to run. What if she ignored the urge to go completely and instead stayed in one place? What if they could only track her movement? What if she defied all her instincts and refused to play the game? They were going to catch her anyway, she was sure of that. So why not make it easier, but not too easy?

She found an old birdbath, the bowl shattered in two, and leaned against the shaft. Above her, water dripped onto the cracked stone. She imagined all the birds that splashed in it once. Imagined their feathers drenched and thinned, the spray of water as they dipped their beaks.

Something tugged at her hair, weak but insistent. She turned and looked up. The bird was not really there. Little more than a memory, but that did not stop it from trying to get her attention. She held out her hand. It was a robin, redbreast little more than a smear of rust. The nematodes that fringed her palm lay to one side, making space for the bird. Once settled, it tucked its head under its wing and went to sleep. She opened her coat and slipped it inside, letting it nest in her pocket.

In the distance she heard the whirlwind scratch of the Sacrifice, the constant chattering of the Calthemites. They were following the past. She glanced around the edge of the birdbath to see where they were. None of them looked toward her, to see her with their plucked-out eyes and shattered sockets. Not wanting to chance it, she dipped back around the birdbath and closed her eyes as the refreshing copper-stained water dripped down the back of her neck and cooled her skin.

Chapter 30
Where Now?

She had to be decisive. Not let the options overwhelm her. She stood and held out her arms once more, letting the nematodes sense the air. They seemed to disagree; then a decision rippled through them from shoulder to wrist. She looked where they were pointing.

"Back where I've just been? Really?"

They did not answer or nod or give any indication of a sentience beyond movement and sensation, but they all continued to point in the same direction.

"I normally don't go with the crowd, but you can't really be called a crowd."

She retraced her steps, checking over her shoulder that the Calthemites were not returning. It did not take her long to find where they had appeared.

Very little remained of Ben. Not much more than his skull and spine, the bone untouched and picked clean. When she brushed her hand over the top, the nematodes craned toward it, stretching like a drowning man beside the shore. She lowered her hand farther and let them brush against his bones.

Without warning, they began to chew through the vertebrae and skull plates, drilled their way through the mineral to the cluster of nerves within and sucked them up until they ran the length of each nematode.

She winced as the ends burrowed into her skin and found her own nerves. In that moment, she saw all that Ben knew. All the times he had entered the Crawl Space. All the tiny grinds of bone and enamel he had sacrificed to visit this no place. She tried to delve through his memories. Search for the reason he returned again and again to the place behind the world.

There were clues. Small hints within the mist of his mind that lurked in those long tangles of nerves. She winced at the taste of whiskey on her tongue and the thoughts from his darker nights when the light outside the window did not reach his mood, and when she saw some of his thoughts about others in the world she wanted to vomit, but still she let the memories flow into her own nerves. Into her own thoughts.

There was a place. He had not told her about it, but there was a place. Or it had been a place. Now it was a ruin, or it would not be here.

She sat down, cross-legged on the ground, knowing that the Crawl Space would protect her from the return of the Calthemites. Closing her eyes, she concentrated on the third place within herself. The place that was neither herself nor the Crawl Space cast in thoughts, but the place that was just Ben. She reached in with sharpened fingers and opened up his memories, letting the nematodes go first and taste the air for traps. There were none.

He had held a map within his head. Held a plan of the Crawl Space. Far more detailed than anything he had told her about. The Mountain of Damp Solidity and the Avenue of Pillars. She saw there were things living under the smashed tiles and walls far more vicious than the nematodes or Calthemites. Far more disturbing than the Sacrifice. She saw creatures with legs made of nothing but roof nails, faces of dropped Stanley knives, blood-stained and ravenous. She saw birds with skin of ash that smouldered and could burn the air from the lungs of anyone nearby, and she saw how to find her way in the Crawl Space. That the ground might be forever changing and shifting, but the ceiling? The ceiling stayed static forever.

She drilled further into his thoughts, tearing through his guilt and his loss and his hangovers, searching for the thoughts he'd hidden deep. Hidden from her and hidden from the Calthemites.

It was disguised as the memory of an excavation. One they'd worked on together. The last day was calm, and then they'd found something in the section. She remembered him calling her over to look at the stains in the wall of soil. The smear of a grave, bones barely visible. They'd worked into the night, the developer's machines coming in the morning. Revealing the grave-cut and the remains, spearhead and shield boss all that remained of the grave-goods so long after death.

She remembered photographing the grave as the sun came up, the site manager coming up and asking them to leave as they needed to get on, and her resisting, telling him exactly what she thought, then taking Ben off to the greasy spoon café for breakfast.

It felt invasive seeing the memory from his angle. Everything was familiar. The scent of the nearby tanning factory, the lights glistening on the trading estate, and the distant noise of revving cars. But something didn't quite fit. She played it over again.

The grave was not a grave. There was no body, just crumbling timbers topping each other, poking out of the dry soil. Keeping her eyes closed, she let the memory play. Watched herself stripping back the topsoil to catch the grave-cut. The taste of whiskey Ben shouldn't have had in his flask. Peering in from the edge of the trench. The feature wasn't a grave, and she knew exactly what it was.

Early hominids was not a subject she ever had to study, but sometimes it was nice to tourist into other eras. The mammoth bones curled out of the soil, their surfaces coated not with dirt, but ochre. They were not upright, but collapsed. Folded in on themselves. Dropped and abandoned. The First Ruin. And as she recognised them for what they were, she knew that this was what Ben was looking for. What the Calthemites were looking for. The centre of the Crawl Space. The heart. The thing that called the rest of the shattered buildings to itself. The First Ruin.

She separated herself from his memories. Returned to the present, opening her eyes and steadying herself against the ground until she was severed from Ben's thoughts and returned to her own.

She knew the direction to head in. She knew what she was looking for, and she knew a shortcut.

Chapter 31
Off the Beaten Track

The Calthemites were not stupid, and it would not take them long to find out she was not following the same path as them. Then they would pursue her once more. But for now, she had an advantage. No expectations. She had no expectation about what the Crawl Space was, and what she could do. She knew it could taste this in her mind. Knew it sensed her naivety, and as it felt this, it opened up the options for her. There were no paths here, just legerdemain and sleight of hand. To not have a direction was more important in a place where there were no directions. She stepped out from the avenue once more.

A mist hung low in the forest, around calf height. She felt it brush against her skin and the nematodes drink, sensing the flavours in the air. She let them get their fill, flinching as the tastes blossomed on her tongue.

She paused and stared above her head at the wooden beams supporting floorboards above. They did not run in the same direction and not all were the same size, but the beams were all aligned in the same direction, and if she was right, if Ben had been right, then they aligned with the First Ruin. The centre of the Crawl Space, the dense point to which all other ruins were attracted.

The mist rose against her legs up to waist height, obscuring the ground below. She tried to brush it out of the way so she could see where to place her feet, but the mist did not comply. Instead, it thickened, and she slowed to make sure each footstep was with care.

To keep herself anchored, she moved from shattered lamppost to broken ecclesiastical pillar, each movement designed to obscure and hold her in one place.

The mist continued to rise.

Something in the Crawl Space side of her brain recognised it for what it was. She started running. The mist began to solidify into glass and splinters. She felt the cuts opening up, dragging on her clothes and skin.

She ran faster, not caring about the ground anymore, trusting her footing and trusting the nematodes to keep her alive.

They were panicked. She felt them pump adrenaline into her, encouraging her to move. Several were sliced from her limbs, and she flinched as they were sliced to pieces. In the distance, the ground rose away from the pillars. Away from the mist. She was running flat out, chunks of glass catching in her breath, blood collecting on her lips. Each step took her farther from the mist, from the sherds of wire-threaded safety glass. She felt the topography change underfoot, rise up away. The mist stopped where it was and started to sink back down into the ground. She rested her head on her knees and spat out nests of fibreglass and gobbets of blood. Where they hit the ground, new nematodes shuffled to life and crawled back, attaching themselves to her wounds. She winced while they anchored themselves to the cuts, the powdered brick and glass pushing into her muscle.

There was a difference between those that held Ben's nerves and those that were all her own. She felt them respond in different ways. Slower and more distracted. Now safe from the mist, she wondered if it was intending to kill her or arm her. Not injurious, but surgical. Then new nematodes were sharp to the touch, edged with blades of window glass and fragments of metal. She flexed them and felt them slash the air. There was more here than neutrality. Even the bombsite still existed in the mind.

With the weight of parasites she now carried, walking was slow and her progress up the hill took time. Below her, the forest retreated to pinpoints, and her back pressed against the floor once more.

Footsteps echoed above her. Snatches of conversation and the sound of coffee cups emptied and washed. Temptation got the better of her. She reached up and hammered on the timber with her fist.

"Can you hear me? I'm down here. Under the floor."

There was a pause in the activity.

"Ssshh. Did you hear that? Under the floor."

"It'll be cockroaches again. We need to get the pest control in. Can you give them a ring?"

"Can't you? I hate talking to him."

The conversation faded away, leaving Rachael on her own with her back pressed against the splintered wood and no way to reach the other side.

Chapter 32
This Place Will Have You Spitting Blood

Not for the first time, she was lost, with only one direction to go. To go on. To keep driving on and ignore all the distractions. She felt oddly alone too, though she carried Ben's memories with her, and was normally okay with her own company. Closing her eyes, she felt the part of her mind that now belonged to the Crawl Space, and the part that held Ben's thoughts. There were no new ones being generated. Just the old static ideas he'd hidden from her.

They tasted different. The Crawl Space part of her tasted of dust and mildew, that which was once Ben whiskey and cheap cigarettes. She wondered about Herr Bettelmein. Was he really behind the Calthemites, or was that a lie that Ben had told her? She searched his memories, but they were incomplete. Fractured. Some were complete, others altered. She could not trust them, apart from that single glimmer of the hidden heart.

The crawl carried on so she could only barely lift her head to see where she was going, rolling forward on Victorian bottles and broken tiles. She no longer cared about injuries, knowing that the nematodes would patch her up, make sure she could keep on going.

On the other side of the crawl, the ground was covered in sheets of lino and abandoned rolls of wallpaper. She ignored them and picked up one of the offcuts, looked at the slope down, and made a decision.

By hooking her feet into a fold at the front, she could control the direction she went, turning to the right and the left at will, avoiding blocks of concrete and old abandoned toilets, until she reached the bottom and came to a stop.

The area widened into what looked like a field, plant-like growths erupting from the ground. She leaned in close to one. Rather than petals, each flower was made of corrugated material, pollen blue and fibrous. She moved the bloom and the powder landed on her hand. From out of nowhere, a gust of air blew the material into her face and she felt it go into her mouth. As it passed her tongue, she knew where she recognised it from. Asbestos. The tiny razor-sharp hairs tore through her lungs, cutting paths that should not exist. There was no way to cough them up. To evacuate them. Around her the breeze became gusts, stripping the flowers of their harvest, coating her lips and nose until there was nothing she could do but swallow down the pollen, each mouthful robbing her of more and more air. The nematodes panicked. Tried to detach themselves. Reach her mouth and evacuate her lungs. Absorb the asbestos. But there was no way. She felt consciousness retreating and slumped to the ground. Something caught her. She turned. The Sacrifice smiled and picked her up in its arms as she fell into a deep suffocating sleep.

Chapter 33
Sprinkled

The floor was still directly above. Much farther above. Rachael closed her eyes once more. The air smelled of cement powder and ash. Vast petals of burnt paper fluttered and settled to stain skin and stone alike.

"Don't sit up. You'll be far more comfortable where you are."

The voice was far away and granulated.

Rachael ignored the advice and sat up.

"I don't think I'll be listening to you. I'm sure you'll understand."

"I'm sure you'll understand if you don't have a choice."

The bricks arced through the air, hitting her in the legs and arms, forcing her back to the ground. She turned her head left and right, trying to ignore the bruises erupting through her skin.

A circle of plaster arced all the way around her, letters spelled out in the same material, distorted from her unnatural angle.

"Your cooperation in this process would make everything easier, Frau Jenson."

The voice was rich and slow, because he had no need to rush.

"Ben said you couldn't be here, Herr Bettelmein."

"And your deceased colleague was right, but there are more ways to manifest than corporeally."

She reached out to the circle and ran her fingers through the powder, flinching as it began to burn.

"Pure slaked lime, Frau Jenson. Of course that's not the purpose of the circle. Merely a side effect."

She turned her head. One of the Calthemites stood slightly separately, their outline distorted by wire mesh and shattered cobbles, giving the silhouette of her employer.

"I can't go anywhere. Can I at least have the dignity of sitting up?"

There was a whisper of conversation like the dying of wasps.

"You may sit up, but don't try and stand."

She didn't let on that there was no way she could. One of the bricks had glanced a blow off her knee and at that moment there was no way she felt it could support her weight.

Her first instinct was right. She sat in the centre of a vast circle made from white powder. The symbols around the edge were unfamiliar, but she did not need to read them to get the implication.

"To keep something out, or something in?"

"Oh, very definitely to keep something in, and not you. You are easy to subdue."

The Calthemites stood some way off, clustered into small groups, piles of rubble by their feet. She spotted Peter amongst the crowd, his face distorted and jaws crumbling the brick dust forming his teeth.

"You see, we have a problem, Frau Jenson." The Calthemite wearing Bettelmein's outline stepped forward. "We need the location of the First Ruin, and we think you now have it. Your colleague had it previously, but the Sacrifice took a rather brutal approach to finding the information. Dissection isn't always the best approach to revealing hidden knowledge."

Rachael shook her head.

"I know nothing. I was running. Running from them. Running for my life, for what it's worth. You can unleash the Sacrifice on me, or Peter over there. There's no occult facts here for them to discover."

Bettelmein's avatar laughed, shedding clay and mortar.

"I have other tools than the Sacrifice," he said, turning to the rest of Calthemites. "Please prepare for the arrival of the Interrogator. Do not worry, Frau Jenson. There will be no more bricks thrown at you. What is coming is far worse."

The circle began to smoke and churn. In the distance, the Calthemites arranged themselves and began to chant. Something nearby was anticipating their words, waiting for them to call it into manifestation. Rachael couldn't tell if it was in the air or in the rubble beneath her, but she could tell it was coming. A needle that would hurt and not cure you. A road crash you could not avoid. Finding the dead body of a loved relative with the words you wanted to speak to them still on your tongue. There was an inevitability to what was arriving and it drained all the fight from her.

She tried to block out their words and the glisten of the slaked lime as it self-combusted. Tried to focus inward and find something to put up a barrier, but nothing remained. In desperation for a distraction, she sifted the pebbles of brick and wall through her fingers, letting them fall to the ground.

A piece of dirt with a fuzz of red spraypaint stuck to her hand, and no matter how hard she shook, the concrete did not detach. Now her eyes saw the red everywhere. Beyond the burning circle, the chanting continued, in snatches of German, English, and several languages she did not recognise. The shifting tone made her want to vomit. Clearing a space by her feet, she laid out the fragments of graffiti, not putting them in any kind of order. Just letting them be in proximity to each other. Letting them accrete and sort themselves out.

The graffiti resolved into the word *Hilflos*, the memory following of a crowd attaching ropes to a wall and pulling it to the ground through the cold.

She concentrated on that image and fed the thoughts to her nematodes. They chewed the concentration into thin strands, excreting them across the rubble. She closed her eyes and saw the world around her through their teeth. The chanting was too distant now.

Around her, the air filled with a grinding sound, but something in the nematodes' industriousness kept her calm. She did not look, apart from in the texture and segments of the worms that were as much a part of her as her own skin.

The chanting increased in volume and intensity, breaking through her concentration, then stopped. The air around her had changed from not present to stifled. She opened her eyes.

The wall extended all the way around her, cloaking her in a cylinder of concrete, graffiti marked and pick-axe scarred. Above her the only thing visible was the underside of the floor that covered all of the Crawl Space.

Outside the wall, something scraped and battered the concrete. Where it dragged along the surface, frost blossomed on the inside, falling down as razors. Avoiding the patches of cold, Rachael pressed her ear against the stone and listened.

"Get it broken down."

"But we can't cross the circle, Herr Bettelmein. If we do, the ghost will cross out into the Crawl Space." She recognised Peter's voice, even through his reshaping.

"And?"

"I know that it won't affect you at such a distance, but once it is out, we can't control it. We just need to be patient. Her defences will not hold forever. The cold will find a way through."

"We do not have time. Her colleague knew the location of the First Ruin and we do not. We need that information. Send some of the worshippers into the circle to break down the wall."

"That's not a good idea, Herr Bettelmein."

There was a silence that was an answer, and then the sound of scorching as someone crossed the burning line. There was again a moment of silence, and then the sound of metal against bone and screaming.

There was no way out. The wall created a cylinder which held the Crawl Space at bay, but gave nowhere for her to escape to, even if she could get past the flaming barrier of slaked lime. Her only chance was to focus on the nematodes holding Ben's severed nerves, and hope there was a clue within them.

She closed her eyes and let her thoughts sink into his memories, follow the strings of sounds and scents, plunge headlong into his knowledge about the Crawl Space.

What erupted in her imagination was not a vision, but a trail of scent. A scent she recognised from working on urban sites. Sometimes pockets of air became trapped in voids between soil and stone, becoming tinted with an odour like petrol. It was distinct from rot or pollution and was often momentary and passing.

She knew what to search for. What to find. She began to dig. With no trowel or mattock, she used her bare hands, clawing out the shattered bricks and sheets of aluminium below where she sat.

There was not much room, but she had worked in worse. Digging out an old post-mediaeval well. Scooping out deep ditch sections, constantly refilling with oil-stained groundwater. With no real light, she worked by touch and scent, searching for the void she knew would be there. Knew would be below her feet.

The ground crumbled away from her bleeding fingers. The space was not much wider than her, and barely big enough to lower herself into. Above her head she heard the conjuration stamping at the ground, trying to get leverage against the wall. She slid herself farther into the gap, shuffling around so she was head-first. Above her, the conjuration gained purchase against the wall, the frost shearing off large chunks of masonry that fell above her, sealing her underground. She stilled her breathing and waited.

The ground erupted in a tremor as the wall spiralled in on itself, collapsing directly on the place where she had so recently sheltered. Above her, she could not make out all the sounds, but the screams were clear, even through the muffle of noise. There was no way back, only forward. A crawl through the dirt and the dust, hoping upon hope that the void she was in did not collapse too soon or, in turn, collapse upon her.

The rest of the wall collapsed. She felt it spiral down to dust above her, sealing her in once and for all.

Chapter 34
Cocooned

The walls of the void were smeared with oil-stained clay, a mixture that transferred its taint to her skin. She crawled on, trying not to think about the weight of a world directly above her. One that could collapse and crush her at any moment.

There were no signs that she was ever going to see the surface. The tunnel continued, with broken tile protruding on all sides that snagged and cut. What she did notice was the lack of vegetation around her. No roots or rotting leaves to drape soil across her eyes. Little damp or smell of decay.

The phrase "the First Ruin" continued to snag her thoughts. She settled her breathing and sought out the nematodes wearing Ben's nerves, groping around for the memory of that single site and the things that should not be there.

As before, the site was exactly as she remembered, apart from the replacement of the grave with the oldest house. The oldest ruin.

How would Ben hide information for himself to find again? To keep it from the Calthemites, but somewhere not too obscure that she would not find it if she needed to?

The mammoth tusks protruded through the subsoil and topsoil, but most of the collapsed structure was hidden by dirt.

She examined the ivory of the tusks and the surface of the bone, looking for any carvings he might have made, but that seemed too obvious. Too easy for the Calthemites to discover if they found this memory, and while they may not straight away understand Ben's notations, they would be able to decrypt them in their own time.

No, he would have done something for himself. She looked around the trench: the half-sectioned features filling with rainwater, and context labels held in place by rusting nails. She pulled one free from the trench edge and stared at the weather-blurred letters, looking for some inspiration, then glanced back over her shoulder toward the vast bone shelter.

The tool hut was where it had been in real life, just off to one side from the two main trenches. The mattocks were rusted as if they had been waiting since the last excavation for her to return. She found the one which didn't have a loose handle, dragged out a spade and barrow, and made her way back toward the buried building.

Time passed in pulses, accelerating through some tasks and slowing for others. There was no night or day to track the shift, no fatigue to stop her, but she worked methodically, and slowly lifted and recorded the first bones.

The house was in a deep cut, and as she started to empty it, she noticed the number of cobbles in the backfill. Too many to be coincidence. She tried to remember the site. Remember the number of inclusions. The soil had been clean and sterile. Not even a spray of charcoal. She put the cobbles to one side and continued down.

Once the house had been planned and excavated, she turned her attention to the cobbles once more. They were covered in scratches. The type made by the point of a trowel. Just loose enough to be passed off as an error. Accidental. They were not.

There was an order to them. A way to read them. She expected the location to be first, but it was not. The first pictograms depicted Herr Bettelmein's plan. Showed the First Ruin in his grasp, still within the Crawl Space. Dragging toward it all the buildings and tarmac from the cities of the earth. Showed all the bones piled up, passing through to clog the Crawl Space with the dead, the land left covered in wild fields and woodland, just for the people they chose.

Turning over each one in turn, she knew that the last ones showed the location. The way to get there. They showed the stages necessary. That the control to travel to the heart of the Crawl Space could not be held in one head. It needed two people. She closed her eyes. There was no way for her to know what his intent was.

Sketching the pictograms onto the context sheets as a way to fix them in her mind, she left the memory and returned to the cloying soil. All she could do was keep going forward and wait for a moment to present itself. This required patience, and cunning that Herr Bettelmein possessed bagfuls of.

With broken hands she continued digging forward, waiting for a chance to take the First Ruin far from the hands of Herr Bettelmein. Far from the grasp of the Calthemites. There was no desire to worship the

Crawl Space and the decay and ruin. There was just a desire to strip the world of the urban and create a past that never existed. She could smell the dead bodies on the air.

Chapter 35
Waymarkers

There were waymarkers. Signs that would lead the way to the centre. The floor above the Crawl Space was too broad and too crude. She needed subtle signs and she needed Ben back.

Digging herself out filled her mouth and eyes with brick dust and cement. Turned her hair a grey that she did not ever think it would recover from. Stained her skin with a thousand abandoned homes. But soon she felt the air above her and pulled herself up onto the floor of the Crawl Space.

There was plenty of detritus around. It didn't matter what she used, she was sure of that, but the finer the better. Cupping her hands together, she carried scoop after scoop of pulverised brick and breezeblock, pulped wallpaper and old tabloids used to cover windows, placing them in a pile until it stood as high as she did.

One by one she tore away the nematodes containing Ben's severed nerves and let them crawl off her hand onto the pile. She felt the severing of something else. The separation from his thoughts and memories, and for a moment she felt it as loss.

The nematodes crawled around, lost and directionless. One by one she pushed them toward the heart of the pile, and then, placing her arm against the pile so her own parasites could burrow in too, she held in her mind a memory of Ben.

It was imperfect, but so was any shape that would emerge from the raw material. She tried to remember the shape of his jaw and the scent of alcohol on his breath. The way he shaped his words, and his gait, letting all her own memories trickle down through her nematodes.

The thing that emerged was incomplete and barely held together by the raw nerves that had spread out, moistening the dust to a type of loose clay. He stepped forward, shuddering away the excess.

"You found the memory?" The words sounded dusty too. Decayed and too slow. She winced and hoped the thing that was Ben did not notice.

"You meant me to?"

"You'll have to carry most of the map. The route. I only have a little space left now in my nerves. A little space to hold a thought."

"Why couldn't I have just left the nematodes attached and carried your half like that?"

"The map needs to be torn. It needs to be broken to fix the route through the Crawl Space. Otherwise the route will just change. Do you understand?"

Cement tipped out of his mouth as he spoke, his eyes the same orbs of rust as when he was alive.

"I understand," Rachael said. "Everything has to be damaged here in some way, to help it find a new purpose. Redemption."

The thing that was Ben shook its head.

"There is no fixing things here. No purpose. No redemption. The Crawl Space does not repair or reunite. It is nothing. It's where the abandoned things go when they leak through between the concrete sheets or get carted off in the skip. There is nothing here that can be redeemed. Including me and you."

"Shall we go?" she said, not rising to the accusation in every sentence he had just said.

"Stand back-to-back with me."

She did as he asked.

"Now close your eyes and concentrate. Can you see the route?"

And she could. It was a verdigris line that snaked in and out between their thoughts leading toward the First Ruin.

"What do we do when we find it?"

The thing that was Ben stayed silent for a moment.

"We destroy it," he said.

"And what happens to something when it gets destroyed here?"

"It goes down to the next level of the Crawl Space."

"And us?"

"We follow it, and when we find it again, we destroy it once more, and keep on until the Calthemites and Herr Bettelmein can no longer possess it."

"And if we get destroyed in the process?"

"Maybe we go down to the next level."

"Don't you know? I saw you torn apart until the only part of you that remained was a shredded cluster of nerves."

"But those shredded nerves survived. Enough for you to find the First Ruin hidden within them. We need to find it in real life now. Hold out your hand."

She did as he asked. Nematodes segmented from pure brick erupted through his skin and searched out hers, the mouths of them locking together. She felt the jolt as the link of the map shifted from something that existed in a thought between them to something that would lead them through the Crawl Space.

"We have the map, but no landmarks to tie in to."

"No need," he said, gesturing forward.

The ground shuddered; rotted copper piping thick with crusted limescale and uric acid rose through the rubble to lie on the surface. In some places it changed to rotten cable, in others barely more than a few flakes of verdigris, the severed hand of a garden ornament. A handful of forgotten low-denomination coins. All led the way from where they were toward the First Ruin.

Chapter 36
Follow the Narrow Blue Road

They walked in silence, their spliced arms moving in unison as they followed the route laid out in front of them. Rachael glanced back. Each flake and pipe returned out of sight as they passed farther on their way.

"It's not staying."

"We're creating the direction, and when we've gone, so do the waymarkers."

Rachael knew she should wait for the right time for the next question, but also knew there was no right time.

"Are you dead?"

"It's complicated," Ben said. "I'm still living, but only in those nerves that you maintained. Will I live outside here? Probably not. Will I live for long inside the Crawl Space? The Crawl Space doesn't have much time for life. We shall see what happens."

They came to a stop at a bank of household waste. Mattresses and bicycles stacked against old lamps and broken furniture. Stacks of newspapers bundled into hoarder's bales. The thin line of copper flakes reached the slope and disappeared.

"The path ends, and it's not here."

Ben shook his head, sending a shudder of plaster across Rachael.

"The line continues, but we just can't see it yet."

Picking up several piles of local free papers, he hauled them out of the way, throwing them behind him. Each stack threatened to topple forward as he forced it apart, but his lack of concern reassured Rachael. Slowly but surely a cavity opened up behind, smelling of papier-mâché and stagnant water.

"These things are rare here, and the water is dangerous. Follow me, don't pull away, and ignore everything, even my voice, until we get to the other end."

"What is it?"

"Nothing but death and misery. Mundane and enduring."

She followed him in.

The walls were slick with water, and somewhere deeper inside she heard the drip of water from the ceiling. A steady, regular pulse of liquid, and something else behind. An electrical pulse, measuring a human one. She kept pace with Ben, ignoring the stench of rot, richer and sweeter than paper.

Her granddad's death had been announced to the wider world with a one inch by one inch box in the local free paper. His death had been announced to her by the stilling of the machines monitoring the blood pulsing through his limbs.

She remembered the smell most of all. There was the hint of full-strength cigarettes he had refused to stop smoking, even as the tumours crowded out any breath in his lungs, and the sweetness of hair lacquer he'd used even as he was catheterised, and cannulated, and radiated. But there was something else. Another sweet scent. A rot, as if he was crystallising. Turning to sugar. She smelled it again now, seeping out from between the pages of the decayed newspapers to either side. The piss-softened mattresses stacked up between them.

The voice came in cascades of waste.

"Dearly beloved. We are gathered here today to honour the memory of." Pause. "Stanley Jenson. Beloved father and grandfather, who will be sorely missed by all who knew him."

The pause was no creation, but a memory. The officiate not even bothering to memorise the name beforehand so it would flow as part of the insincere memorial he delivered.

She brushed against a stack of papers and something fell out from between the pages.

"Wait," she said, kneeling to pick them up.

The photos had once been on her father's mantelpiece. Family photos of her grandfather holding her dad when he was a baby. Standing beside her grandma whom she never knew. She held them up to get a better look.

The mildew was very precise, only obscuring the faces. Turning smiles into gaping chasms where there were no features, no pleasant memories. Just voids and loss. She let them drop from her hand and tried to focus on the incessant drag of the nematodes attached to what used to be her friend. But if there were those photos amongst the papers, there might be more. Letters or notes, even. She remembered his perfect handwriting, loop upon loop that helped her fall in love with words. If she just paused for a few moments to look, to examine the gaps between. They must have been brought here together. Kept together. Maybe she could find his birth certificate, or love letters that were meant to have been lost.

She held her stance and did not move. Let her fingers move through the sheets of damp paper. In the background, the sound of the IV drip got louder. Broadsheets and tabloids fell apart against her touch, tears of adverts landing on her hand. No more photos or letters. She looked down at her wrist. The paper now covered her forearm and she tried to move away. It had hardened. Solidified. The air filled with the scent of wet flour and wallpaper paste. The papier-mâché was setting upon her skin while it crept up her arm toward her elbow. She could watch it travel in real time like an unchecked infection. Nervous, she reached over with her other arm, the one welded to the thing that used to be Ben, and tried to prise herself free. Her fingers stuck to the surface and glistened as the papier-mâché engulfed that too, slid across her skin and the brick-dust flesh of Ben. There was no way to free herself. She was trapped here in the rot of the past by her memories.

Chapter 37
Encased

Rachael was encased, but not alone. Ben, or what remained of him, had been compressed to a paste along one side of her body, the papier-mâché holding him in place. She felt the now hardened paper pressing each grain of dust and plaster to indent her skin, a sensation that crawled across her skin. Outside of her containment she heard voices.

"Are you still there?" she whispered. There was a shifting along one side.

"I am, but I can't do much to get us out."

"Do you think it's the Calthemites outside?"

There was a pause that pressed out and flexed the solid paper prison which coated her skin.

"It's possible." His voice was the tumble of dirt down a slope. "But we still need to get out and take our chances."

She felt like a bird, shell hemmed, though at least a bird had space to twist around before it pecked its way to the air.

"How can I breathe?"

"The nematodes would find a way."

Hearing their name, she felt them twitch against her skin, their extremities outside the hardened paper.

"Can they see?"

"All nematodes are blind," Ben's scratching voice said, somewhere in the back of her head. "But they can increase themselves."

She felt the truth in what he said.

"I can't help you," he continued, and she knew the truth in this too.

The nematodes did not think. They were not independent. They were extensions of her but separate. Joined but detached.

"Think of them like your stomach biome. You can't control them or order them, but you can influence them."

She let her mind settle. Found the places at the margins where the nematodes attached to her. Ran her thoughts along the roots where they were anchored within her muscles.

The nematodes began to seek. Thinned themselves, stretching out into the obscure outside. She felt them drag grains to themselves, widen their bodies. If the figures outside noticed, they paid no attention. As the nematodes increased themselves, the paper started to creak at the pressure. There seemed to be no resistance from the encasement. Crack by crack and crease by crease it fell to the nematodes' maturing at the suggestion of Rachael.

The cracks that formed through the once sodden paper spread and joined until she saw light coming through above herself. The air was different, even though she had no need to breathe. No one tried to stop the opening. No one tried to stop the emergence. The papier-mâché fell away, the nematodes now vast, so heavy that one whole side of her body hung down under the weight.

She lay still and turned her head. Several people stood a distance away, their backs turned, circling on the Sacrifice. Up close, the thing that had once been a person had nothing left that did not come from the Crawl Space. Limbs of steel reinforcement, skin of broken concrete. Hair, what there was of it, twisting and flexing as if it had life of its own.

Tumbles of plaster fell from its face, slid down to the ground, and erupted back up in white clouds that stained her skin to a ghost.

It noticed her. Pulsing in size as it moved across to where she lay, it stepped carelessly, each press of its feet against the ground dragging more dust and brick into itself, rebars clattering against each other. Stood over her, it leaned close. Its breath smelled of dried urine and the rot of cement bags on an abandoned building site.

Rachael stared into its eyes, searching for a trace of humanity, even as she doubted the remnants of her own.

"What are you?"

Fingers of splinters brushed against the tips of her nematodes and she felt them flinch at the skin that was not skin.

"I am Bettelmein. I am the thing that eats every last inch of your skin and leaves you wrapped in nothing but the memory of pain."

Chapter 38
Sacrifice

She heard Ben's words.

The only way a rich man can move into the Crawl Space is to sacrifice everything.

There was nothing left of the man who had, until recently, been her employer. Nothing underneath the dust and the tattered fragments of fibreglass. She searched the eyes of shattered windowpanes as long as she dared look, trying to pinpoint a single spark of humanity, but there was none.

"A bit of an extreme step."

"Extreme endeavours require extreme actions, Frau Jenson."

"Sacrificing yourself seems a bit far even for you. Don't you have people for that sort of thing?"

"Some jobs are too important to entrust to an inferior."

As he spoke, he changed, flexing in and out as the words issued from him.

"Now you and your barely remnant co-worker are going to create the path to lead us to the First Ruin."

"And if we don't?"

The rebar extended from the Sacrifice's arm, twisted and rusted, the end ground to a jagged point. She braced herself for it piercing her face or her throat. Now she was unsure if she would ever return from this half-world of rubble and rust. It was not like something was going to be taken from her. There was nothing left to take.

The rebar did not stab her, though she was ready for that. Instead it severed through the head of one of her nematodes, the metal spike working its way through the twitching body until it touched the point the worm rooted into her skin.

She watched it dying. Smelled the damp and mildew erupt from within it as the nematode tried to struggle away from the damage being done to it. Tried to save itself. She felt the scrape of the iron ridges as they pinned the nematode to the dirt. The metal clawing down the centre of her spine. A phantom that was all too real.

"You need to create the path for me."

"And if I don't?"

The Sacrifice smiled and wept tears of pure clay as it drove the rebar even farther into the nematode. Rachael watched it wilt and blacken, falling off into the rubble underfoot.

The grief came in a wave. An opaque sadness of change. Of something that could never be fixed. In a place of waste and broken things, the death of this creature that was attached to her, but might not have ever been truly alive, moved through her like smoke, blackening everything with stains that would never scrub clean.

"You feel that grief? You feel that sadness? That overwhelming sense of loss?" The Sacrifice was gloating now. She could not tell if it was just Bettelmein, or if there were others in there with him. "That was just for one of the nematodes. You have forty-seven of the dirty parasites nested into your skin. Imagine what the mourning will feel like when we kill them all, one by one."

"You don't have the patience to do that."

"We have a lot of patience, Frau Jenson. We have waited a long time to find our way here. We needed someone like you. Curious and able to open the way into the Crawl Space, and then lead us through. Now you will lead us to the First Ruin, or we will sever every connection that exists between you and the nematodes until you are little more than a residual hanging off the edge of your less corporeal companion."

The Sacrifice did not remove the first length of rebar as the second extended and severed the next nematode. She tried to hold the dark sense of loss at bay, the charring of mourning that reshaped everything with ash. Then the next and the next, until every glance she took toward the creature that had once been Bettelmein was spotted with burns from her thoughts.

Fourteen nematodes lay dead and pierced on the floor around her. The Sacrifice stood over her, and still she would not give in, even as she balled up the loss and buried it deep, beyond the reach of the Crawl Space, or the Sacrifice, or even Ben, wherever he had gone to.

Ben had been silent all the way through the death of her parasites, and that only intensified the grief. She knew it was for the best. That he was masking himself to protect himself. To stop the Sacrifice from finding a way to him. To stop it teasing him out and maybe attaching Ben to himself, or torturing him to force her to co-operate. And yet it made things so much worse. To be so fucking alone in this place, while the death of those she was attached to intensified around her. To know he was so close but was not there to comfort her.

She knew if she called to him, he would come. Out of loyalty? Out of guilt? Either/or, but he would come, and he would give himself up to get her out of here. But for now, she stayed silent and Ben stayed hidden.

The Sacrifice strode around her, extending the rusted lengths of rebar as it did so.

"You can do what you want," she said, breaking her silence. "I won't give him up."

It was over her in moments, the broken point of the metal pressing against her eyelid, the pressure sending shots of red light through her vision.

"I need your voice to ask for him to return, but I can take so much from you first," it said. "I can sever you from the little humanity you have left, then build you a new body of pain that every movement is a moment of agony. Muscles of splinters and shatters of glass that grind against each other. I can make it so that you never leave and slowly but surely you become one of these."

It reached down and picked up a desiccated nematode, letting the powder fall into her face.

"Your saviour didn't tell you that, did he? That those who lose themselves here become non-corporeal and can only find their way by making simple cylindrical bodies." The Sacrifice picked up another and slowly chewed the dead dust, spitting it back. "These aren't mindless creatures. These are souls that are trapped here and have no way to get home. I will cut everything away from you until there is nothing left but a single thought that can then take up residence in one of these, and then I will chew that to a paste that will coat my throat."

The next length of rebar hit the nematode with such force it vaporised, the brick dust that made it coating everything in fine red powder.

She wept. For the first time since she entered the Crawl Space, she wept, letting her tears hit the floor.

"Your little alcoholic friend left that out. Now, fellow Calthemites, please hold her down."

She did not care anymore. There was nothing inside or outside for her to reclaim. She was little more than a rag and bones. Things to be reused for something no one wants. The next length of rebar severed another nematode, and now she knew why the grief was so intense. The nematodes were part of her, but they also contained a glimmer of those who could not escape this place. They were the simple bodies on the first stage of an evolution that could not evolve.

The knowledge did not lessen the grief and the loss. Another one died in the dust, and the length of twisted metal scraped her arm.

She watched the blood flow into the rubble, and she did not care. Maybe Bettelmein had won. Maybe the battle had been lost a long time ago. When she lost her passion for work. She watched the blood seep away. Another ruin in the land of ruins. That was what she was. There was no way back from this.

One of the nematodes crawled across to plug the gap. The Sacrifice reached down and gripped its neck, holding it back. She did not care enough. She did not care enough anymore to save herself. Her only glimmer of pleasure was that she would rob Bettelmein of his victory.

"You need to stop this."

Ben's voice came from inside her voice, inside her own throat.

"I don't need to stop anything," she said out loud. The Sacrifice looked around at the sound of her words.

"I wasn't talking to you," Ben said, again more inside than outside.

"You don't get to decide that." There was no way that he was going to stop her making this decision. Stop her having control.

"Then let me leave."

She nodded, and as she did, she felt his thoughts slide out into the dirt at her feet, watching him become again.

When he had regained his body, he stood in front of the Sacrifice.

"We will lead you to the First Ruin."

"And her," the Sacrifice said.

Ben looked over at her, and even though it was shaped with dust and splinters, she knew what the expression meant. It meant that she was able to make the decision. That if she said no, he would understand. That she had much more experience than her, but this particular feature, or ditch or grave, he had spent long enough working on that he knew it in detail, and when he said it was Roman or modern or natural, then it was.

"How do we make the path if we're no longer joined?" she said.

"Concentrate."

Chapter 39
Watched

Bringing the path back in front of them was harder now that they were not conjoined. Rachael stood beside Ben, or what was now Ben, and concentrated on finding his thoughts in the mess of the Crawl Space. She concentrated on the colour of verdigris. The particular tones as it flaked and separated. As it detached from the copper piping to collect below. The creation of water and metal. The creation of her thoughts and Ben's.

The path was even fainter this time, barely more than a single line in the dirt, but it was there and it was obvious enough to see. To her and Ben.

"You better not be taking us the wrong way, because I will trap both of you within myself and hold you until every last building on earth has crumbled to dust."

"If you have your way, that won't be too long, Bettelmein," Ben said, his concentration flitting for a moment and the path fading before he returned to the route.

Out of the corner of her eye, she saw the Sacrifice smile.

"The world does not need the people it currently has. It does not need the towns and cities it currently has. There is a purity underneath that needs to be released. An ideal that gives clarity. An idea of fields and woodland. Of small villages."

"That world never existed," Rachael said, trying to hold the image of the route in place while she spoke. "It only exists in imagination. It never lived."

She turned to face the Sacrifice, the path in front flickering and fading as her concentration shifted.

"That's what makes it so powerful," it said. "This world is something to yearn for. An ideal beyond all the detritus and waste. Beyond all the squalling of people and children. All the grasping. It's a world we can make perfect for those who want it."

"For the right people."

"That is a division only seen by those who are on the wrong side. There are people and there is nothing. Maybe you are the right type to come into the idyll, or maybe you belong here amongst the detritus."

Rachael looked the Sacrifice up and down as it barely held onto its form as Bettelmein. How could he say that when he was shaped from broken bricks and iron bars? When he was shaped from the very stuff he wanted to reject? The slew of cities and the life within them.

She felt Ben next to her, his hand resting on her arm, barely holding the concentration to maintain his shape and maintain the thoughts to hold the path in place, but it was there. Glimmering with the sea blue, turquoise, and teal. A single line in the dust and dirt and plaster and rot of abandoned, rusted mattresses. They did not talk, and the link between them was faint now. She walked on in silence, the shared idea of the route the only link. Behind them, the Calthemites followed in procession.

Chapter 40
Closer

Rachael felt the drag of the First Ruin as they got closer. The landscape around them was more mixed. Old wooden huts lay on top of shattered temples. Scorched terminals from longhouses poked out between the cobbles from metalled paths. To the side of where they walked, she saw the blank eyes of statues that were no longer worshipped and middens long forgotten by the dead and their ancestors.

Behind them, the Calthemites began chanting. She turned her head to look. To see what they were doing. All of them wore masks, the fabric flexing as the Nematodes studded their skin. Her own twitched in annoyance of her distraction and she turned back to help conjure the route once more. Beside them, the Sacrifice strode, dragging more and more of the fabric of the Crawl Space to itself.

The ground dipped, tumbling toward the centre. Ben stopped on the edge and Rachael followed suit. The blue path petered out, but there was no need for it now. The First Ruin stood in the centre, vast lengths of mammoth ivory curving up into the sky.

Rachael felt the magnetism. She felt the pull of the centre. The way it slowly dragged the forgotten and the abandoned toward it. Pulled the waste from the living world above, and settled it across the Crawl Space.

She glanced up. The floor was still above them. In most places still planked with rough dressed wood, but directly above the First Ruin, the floor was made of reeds and animal skins. She watched them flex as if someone padded down on them with bare feet, and smelled the hint of water-sodden hides.

The Sacrifice strode forward, down the slope toward the hut, standing on the margin to the ground where it waited.

"It's even more beautiful in real life," and Rachael heard in his voice that he truly believed it. As did she. This was far further back than any building she had ever excavated, but she saw the simplicity and the delicacy of its construction. The selection of the individual hides and the tusks to make it. To stand it on its own. Even as it lay torn and fallen, there was an elegance, and she felt the power that came from it. She glanced down under her feet. The ground was made up of flakes or flint, debitage stretching in all directions. She felt around for the thoughts that were Ben in the vague shape to her side, and nodded toward the stone waste all around. He shifted his attention quickly away.

The Sacrifice continued to stare for a moment at the collapsed hut, then came back to face the waiting Calthemites.

"Prepare the site," it said, and for a moment it flashed with the shape of Bettelmein; then he was gone. She wondered how much of the Sacrifice was him and how much was the Crawl Space.

The Calthemites were slow to move, but once they got going, they fell into their roles like ants, searching through the detritus for treasures Rachael could not recognise. They paid no attention to the flint flakes and cores that spread for miles in all directions. They paid no attention to her or Ben.

Sitting down, she started to sort through the flakes, turning them over in her hand, running her fingers over the smooth, bulbous fractures. There was a beauty to worked stone that she never tired of. The perfect shape of the strike, even in the abandoned flakes. One by one she piled them up beside her.

Below her, the Calthemites were dismantling the First Ruin. Tearing apart the rotten hides with their bare hands and ripping them into strips. Others were collapsing the mammoth tusks and laying them in a circle, white and smooth. In the centre, the Sacrifice walked around, as if he was trying to remember his lines.

The pile of debitage beside her was growing larger as she sorted through them. Some she recognised. Black, almost translucent flint from the coast of Norfolk. But others were more unusual. Obsidian and crystal. Even some bottle glass, chipped and shaped. Occasionally she found a tool abandoned during shaping and turned it over and over, tracing the decisions of the maker. The choices they had made until they could go no further.

That's how she felt now. She could go no further. Any resistance was not going to achieve anything. She was a tool, used and abandoned and of no further purpose. The pile beside her grew bigger. Occasionally she found an oyster shell within the spread and placed it on the edge of the collection.

It brought back memories of training digs, sorting through the finds from a working floor and washing them in cold huts on the edge of wind-creased fields. All that seemed so long ago.

The Sacrifice was moving the Calthemites into place around the collapsed hut. Placing them at specific roles, with one final look up to where she sat beside the remnants of Ben, the Sacrifice began to chant.

She felt the change straight away. The air intensified and compressed down upon her. There was no breath in her lungs, and she felt flattened by the intent in the air. She smelled rosewater and salt glaze. Burning feathers, and somewhere beyond that, the stench of rot.

She turned to Ben. At least that was a familiar presence. There would be nothing left when the ritual finished, but at least knowing he was there could give her something to hold onto.

"Stay here," he said, the voice deep in her head.

What little there was left of her colleague, her friend, was enwrapped around the stack of shattered stone beside her.

"I need your help to shape me."

She nodded and held his outline in her head, letting him fit the flints into place. She knew that he was forgetting himself, becoming dissipated. That there was little of him left. Slowly, as she concentrated, Ben became a thing of blades.

Chapter 41
Severed

Ben was a thing of knives and a thing of blades, and as he moved down the slope toward the Calthemites, he became a thing of death. She felt his thoughts, the connection now stronger as he regained his form, and she felt every single wound he inflicted moving through the worshippers around the circle.

There was no need to fight. Every step he took, every movement of his arm, drew blood. She watched him force his hand down the throats of the Calthemites, rupturing them from within. They were skin and muscle and nerve, and they fell away easily.

One got in a lucky blow, spreading the flakes making up his leg across the floor, but she remembered his shape and brought him back to form, trying not to watch as he dragged his forearm across their throat. Soon the wound through the circle was edged in blood and damage even the nematodes could not repair, but it had taken its toll. He was finding it harder and harder to hold his shape, and she was finding it harder and harder to concentrate.

The Sacrifice barely paid them any attention. It stared toward the floor, and Rachael looked toward what was taking its attention. The floor was bulging down toward them as if a great weight was pressing through, and she knew that when that breach came, then the real world would cascade through.

Ben was shedding the flint. The sheer strain of concentration was too much, and even with her help he was not able to keep form as he tried to breach the circle to get at the Sacrifice.

"Come back to me," she said.

Ben turned and saw her stood there. She stretched out her arms and waited.

"You'll be injured," he said. Even the voice in her head was faint now.

"I'll be worse if we don't try."

He settled upon her, trying to keep the sharpened flint away from her skin, but it was impossible. A thousand tiny cuts opened up across her body and she tried to relax, have faith in the nematodes to repair the wounds.

"Ready?" she said, not knowing if there was enough of Ben left to know what the word meant.

"Ready," he said, as if from a distance.

She walked forward.

A few of the Calthemites were alive on the floor, but none of them tried to prevent her. With the blades draped across her, and her shape giving them form and solidity, she crossed the threshold into the circle. The thing that was Bettelmein and was the Sacrifice turned to face her and Ben conjoined, and laughed.

"You think you can prevent this with some kind of garment? This is primal and ancient and needed," it said, and turned its back.

Rachael walked forward toward the chanting thing, and with one movement walked forward and straight through the Sacrifice, cutting it to ribbons.

Around them, the Calthemites blackened with mildew, and in front of the Rachael/Ben hybrid, the Sacrifice turned to smaller and smaller pieces until there was nothing left apart from a rust-coloured powder that blew away.

Avoiding the chips of flint close to her eyelids, Rachael glanced up at the ceiling. The bulge had disappeared as the ritual faltered and now she stood in the dismantled First Ruin with silence and blades surrounding her.

"Is it over?" she said to no one in particular, but specifically to Ben.

"No," he said. "No, it isn't."

Chapter 42
Waiting

"But nothing is getting dragged through to here," she said, pointing toward the ceiling.

"You're more correct than you think," he said. She felt him peel away, standing before her dressed in knives. "Nothing at all is getting dragged here. Slowly but surely the world will fill up with waste and damage and ruin until there is no space for anyone anymore. The reverse of what Bettelmein was striving for, but just as disastrous."

She looked at the damaged First Ruin and knew that he spoke the truth. The centre of the Crawl Space was gone. There was nothing left to drag the waste and the debitage of the world here. No central point.

"Can it be repaired?"

"No, not without a presence."

"Without a presence?"

Ben stepped into the circle and sat down in the middle of the dismantled ruin.

"I don't know how much I have to work with," he said.

And she watched while he found out, sending thoughts as nematodes into the surrounding rubbish. Trying to find all the torn strips of hide and fragments of tusk.

"This will not hold together on its own."

"You need to come back," she said, reaching out to comfort him, then seeing blades and wincing at the cuts already netting her skin.

"There's not enough of me to go back," he said. "And this is what I wanted."

She backed out of the circle and stood on the margins, feeling the flint crunch under her feet, and stared at the mask of knives that was still her friend.

"I understand," she said.

"What are you going to do?" the new centre of the Crawl Space asked, settling into position in the ruins of the First Ruin.

"Try and find a way back."

"I can help with that."

"I'm going to take my time and explore," she said. "See what I can find."

And as she turned away from Ben, the Creature of Blades, the Centre of the Crawl Space, the Guardian of the First Ruin, she saw him smile and allowed herself the same luxury.

END

Acknowledgements

A book is never completely written in isolation, even if it feels like it sometimes. Huge thanks to Scarlett and the team at JournalStone for bringing *Crawl Space* to life. This one has been sitting as a computer file for a while, and to see it finally as a book means a lot.

To the members of PAWS who have read so much of my work over the years and made me a better writer with their feedback. Thank you to Maria, Sarah, Julie, Carina, Marianne, Kathrin, Karen, and Jordan.

To the British horror community, who have been so welcoming over the years. To my regular dining companions, Freud and Kayleigh, Kit and Kelly. To my dear friend Priya for introducing me to so many good people.

Most of this book was written at home keeping my own company, so I'm incredibly grateful to those people I chat to on a regular basis, particularly Max Gee, Tracy Fahey, and Ella. Especially to Trix for the thirty year long conversation we've been having, which does more to keep me on an even keel than you know.

To all the archaeologists I've worked or studied with over the years, whether that was the HND in Yeovil, digging for the various units around the country, or studying for my MA in Sheffield. This might not seem like an archaeology story at first glance, but it absolutely is, and wouldn't exist without your friendship. A particular shout-out to Dr Stuart Prior and Tim Robinson, who have travelled many of the same roads as me. I'm proud to still call you friends after all this time.

To Dave and Tammy. When we sit down after not seeing each other for a year or two, it always feels like picking up where we left off.

To Mike and Shel, the big brother and big sister I never had.

To the Endicott Studio artists and writers, especially Terri Windling, Ellen Kushner, Delia Sherman, and Charles de Lint. Thank you for showing me that there is magic in the world, and when the world is dark, there are ways to fight. I'm so glad I get to call you my friends

To Annie for being there for so many years, and always encouraging me, even as I chose another highly secure, well paid, career…

And, as always, to Charlie who is the best of me, and as he surpasses me in height will surpass me in talent, intelligence, and kindness. I am immensely proud of you.

About the Author

Steve Toase was born in North Yorkshire, England, and now lives in the Frankenwald, Germany.

Steve's fiction has appeared in *Analog*, *Nightmare Magazine*, *Three Lobed Burning Eye*, *Shimmer*, *Bourbon Penn*, and *Deadlands*, amongst others, and his stories have been selected for Ellen Datlow's *Best Horror of the Year* series and Paula Guran's *Year's Best Dark Fantasy and Horror*.

Steve's debut short story collection *To Drown in Dark Water* is published by Undertow Publications, and his archaeology-themed horror collection *Dirt Upon My Skin* is out now from Black Shuck Books. *Dirt Upon My Skin* was shortlisted for the British Fantasy Award 2025 Best Collection.

He also likes old motorbikes and vintage cocktails.

www.ingramcontent.com/pod-product-compliance
Lightning Source LLC
LaVergne TN
LVHW051009080826
845145LV00009B/2523

9781685101749